Diane Warner's
Great Parties
on Small Budgets

Diane Warner's
Great Parties
on Small Budgets

Celebrations for Grownups and Kids of All Ages

by
Diane Warner

New Page Books
A division of Career Press, Inc.
Franklin Lakes, NJ

DIANE WARNER'S GREAT PARTIES ON SMALL BUDGETS
EDITED BY DIANNA WALSH
TYPESET BY JOHN J. O'SULLIVAN
Cover design by Lu Rossman/Digi Dog Design
Printed in the U.S.A. by Book-mart Press

To order this title, please call toll-free 1-800-CAREER-1 (NJ and Canada:
201-848-0310) to order using VISA or MasterCard, or for further information on books from Career Press.

The Career Press, Inc., 3 Tice Road,
PO Box 687, Franklin Lakes, NJ 07417
www.careerpress.com
www.newpagebooks.com

Library of Congress Cataloging-in-Publication Data

Warner, Diane.
  Diane Warner's great parties on small budgets : celebrations for grownups and kids of
all ages / by Diane Warner.
    p. cm.
  ISBN 1-56414-613-8 (paper)
    1. Entertaining. 2. Parties. 3. Cookery. I. Title: Great parties on small budgets. II.
Title.

TX731 .W353 2002
793.2—dc21   2002019882

588 0345

Dedication

To my Mom, Michelle Sparr.
Thank you for
your love and encouragement
through the years.

Acknowledgments

My sincere thanks go to my daughter, Lynn Paden; my daughter-in-law, Lisa; and my many friends in Tucson, Arizona, who shared their creative ideas for this book. I'd like to especially thank Jo Yoder, Connie Nelson, Raquel Cook, Marlene Fox, Mickie Harris, and my neighbors, George and Marilyn Eddington, who so graciously provided the French translations for the Cruise Ship Formal Night Dinner.

I would also like to thank my agent, Jeff Herman, and several important people at Career Press/New Page Books, including Ron Fry, Anne Brooks, Mike Lewis, John O'Sullivan, Dianna Walsh, Stacey Farkas, Clayton Leadbetter, and Jackie Michaels.

Thank you all for contributing to the success of this book.

Contents

Introduction

This book has been a lot of fun to write. What a concept: a great party on a small budget! We've needed this book for a long time.

Part 1 of this book presents the basics for entertaining on a small budget, from affordable party invitations to decorations and fun for children, teen, and adult parties.

In addition to the basics, Parts 2 through 4 provide affordable themes for birthday parties, holiday parties, and special occasion parties, where everything you need to host the party is not only budget-minded, but specific, including theme-related invitations, costumes, decorations, fun stuff, and party fare.

Part 5 presents affordable, yet tasty and creative, recipes for all kinds of parties, from children's to adults', including beverages, snacks, appetizers, and formal and informal fare. You'll enjoy perusing these recipes, and I'm sure you'll find just the right menu for your party.

Finally, I've included in Part 6 small-budget party worksheets that will not only keep you organized as you plan the party, but will help you stay on budget.

Although I've been planning affordable parties all my life, I was still amazed with the clever, creative ways parties are being put together these days. Even families going through difficult economic times are finding ways to throw awesome birthday parties for their kids, joyous holiday parties, and memorable special occasion parties. And how are they doing this, you ask? Well, they're improvising by using things they already have around the house; they're shopping wisely at discount stores; and they're opting for affordable themes, such as the "Peeper Family Puppet Party" that uses empty tissue boxes and inexpensive garden gloves; a "Wine-Tasting Party" where the guests provide the wine for tasting; or an Engagement Party where the emphasis is on free-as-air nostalgia and heart-tugging toasts.

I hope you enjoy the creative, affordable ideas gleaned for this book. As you try them out, I'll bet this book becomes a "keeper."

Part

Small-Budget Party Basics

This section presents basic ideas for hosting an affordable party, including the invitations, decorations and party fun. These are general ideas that can be used for all kinds of parties, many of which draw from things you already have around the house or inexpensive props that can be purchased at dollar stores or your favorite discount market.

Specific theme-oriented ideas are presented in the theme parties that follow this section, but the basic ideas found here can be used for a variety of party themes.

Small-Budget Invitations

The best place to begin cutting costs is with the invitations. Most people go to the store, purchase a package of invitations, fill in the blanks, and mail them. Not only are there more economical ways to invite your guests, but more creative ways as well.

Here are a few commonsense basics for small-budget invitations:

- Computer-generate your invitation using your clip art or graphics programs. Send it as an e-mail attachment or print it out to be faxed.
- Invite your guests in person or over the telephone.
- Save postage by hand-delivering your invitations.
- If you prefer to mail your invitations, save on postage by creating postcard invites.
- Whether you have access to a computer printer or not, you can always create one clever master invitation, complete with clip art or a photo of the honored guest, then copy it onto heavy stock color paper at your local copy center.
- Send a customized e-card invitation.
- Create an affordable customized invitation using the computer-generated card services available at many greeting card stores.
- For a children's birthday party, have the birthday child create a master invitation on a sheet of paper using crayons; then have him "decorate" the invitation with his artwork. Once you have the master, you can either scan it on your computer scanner and make color copies, or make copies at your local copy store.

- Make copies of the honored guest's photo; print the invitation on the back and mail.
- Speak or sing the invitation onto a cassette tape; duplicate onto inexpensive tapes. Hand-deliver or mail.
- Roll up a computer-generated invitation and insert it inside a Cracker (aka "Popper") and hand-deliver it. (See Chapter 3 for Cracker-making directions.)
- Hand-print the invitations on heavy construction paper or light poster board, and cut to the size you want them to be. Convert the invitation into a jigsaw puzzle by cutting each into six or eight pieces. Mail the pieces in envelopes. Of course, the recipients will have to assemble the puzzle in order to read the invitation.
- Make "admission ticket" invitations: cut poster board into 2-1/2 inch x 6 inch "tickets." Use a real ticket as your guide, including the words "Admit One to a Party" in honor of David Bronson's 10th birthday, for example. Include the rest of the party details on the ticket, perforate the edges with a one-hole punch, enclose in an envelope, and mail.
- Wanted Poster invitations: Create a realistic Wanted Poster that includes a photo of the honored guest as one of FBI's Most Wanted and the crimes committed, such as "caught stealing Mother's cookies," and "last seen trailing cookie crumbs down hallway carpet," and so forth. Be sure the poster states that there is a large "REWARD" for anyone who meets at (place of party) on (date and time of party), along with other party details. Mail in large envelopes or hand-deliver.
- Purchase fluorescent poster board (aka Day Glo) and cut it into shapes that complement your theme, such as a pumpkin for a Halloween party, a baby bottle for a baby shower, or a dog for a Petting Zoo party. Write your invitation on the cut-outs and mail.
- Create an "invisible invitation" by placing one piece of paper on top of another. Use a ball-point pen to print the invitation on the top sheet, pressing down *hard*. The letters will leave impressions on the second sheet, which you mail to your guests. Each guest must lightly color over the letters, using a pencil or crayon, and presto! The words come to life! This idea works great for children's parties.

Small-Budget Decorations

ou can create a festive ambience for your party by using items or materials you already have around the house, by purchasing low-cost supplies, or by choosing a theme that lends itself to free or economical decorating. For example, all you need for a Teddy Bear Party are dozens of teddy bears, which are surprisingly easy to round up.

Every theme-oriented party described in this book includes suggestions for low-cost decorations. However, here are a few basic ideas for small-budget decorating:

- **Everyday Items:** Decorate by using items you already have around the house or that you can borrow from friends and family. For example, borrow patio furniture for a garden party; tiki torches for a luau; or topiaries or houseplants that can be dressed up for the party with ribbons, lights, or theme-related accessories.

- **Table Art:** Think of your tabletop as a canvas; you're the artist and it's up to you to "paint" an appealing picture for your guests. Start with an interesting, yet affordable, table covering, such as a bed sheet, layered place mats, or scrunched-up fabric remnants from your local fabric store. Then add items you already have on hand to make the table interesting, such as your collection of Hummel figurines, antique bottles, toy trains or cars, salt and pepper shakers, or other mementos, artifacts, or collectibles you may have accumulated from your travels. Fruit and flower arrangements also work well, especially if they are freely available from your garden.

19

- **Theme-Related Place Mats:** Create an original, theme-related place mat, then copy it at your local copy shop. For example, for an engagement party, wedding rehearsal dinner, or anniversary party, enlarge a photo of the couple and copy it onto 8 1/2 x 11inch sheets. You can use these sheets as is or cover them by laminating or with clear contact paper. These place mats can then be given to the guests as take-home mementos of the party.

- **Balloons:** The biggest bang for any party buck is the use of plain, ordinary balloons; they don't have to be helium-filled. Just blow them up, tie them at the necks with colorful crinkle-tie ribbon and suspend them from the chandelier, set in shallow bowls around the party area, or attach to doorways and stairways. Balloons are festive and create an instant party feeling to your venue. Note: Whenever I mention balloons throughout this book, it's an important precaution to never allow children to blow them up because there is the danger of sucking them into their throats and choking—adults only!

- **Crepe Paper:** Purchase sheets of crepe paper and cut them into strips yourself, or you can purchase rolls of pre-cut strips. Suspend crepe paper strips from the ceiling or chandelier over the serving table to create a canopy by attaching the strips to the corners of the table.

- **Candles:** If appropriate, add as many as you can afford to your party venue; they create an enchanting ambience, especially after dark. Look for sales at party supply stores, discount stores, and dollar stores. Place the candles in candleholders or theme-related containers, such as glass jars (tied with ribbon at their necks), small clay gardening pots, or wine glasses.

- **Strings of Tiny White Lights:** White Christmas tree lights can be used any time of year to help produce a magical setting for an evening get-together. Hang them over doorways and windows; wrap them around silk trees or plants; or trail them down the center of your serving table.

- **Luminaries:** Luminaries say "welcome" to your guests as they arrive for your evening party. They are inexpensive and easy to make: fill ordinary brown or colored paper lunch bags with three inches of sand and set a lighted votive candle inside each one.

- **Ice Lanterns:** Ice lanterns are an interesting variation of the lunch sack luminary. They are created by freezing water in 36-ounce coffee cans, creating blocks of ice. Loosen the blocks of ice by running warm water over the coffee cans, then chip a hole in the top of each ice block and insert the candles. They're especially effective in the winter when placed in the snow that lines the walkway or entry way to your home.
- **Butcher Paper:** White or colored butcher paper can be used in a number of ways to decorate your setting. It can serve as a tablecloth by decorating with theme-related stickers or cut-outs, or it can be customized by providing the guests with felt-tip markers to write messages to the guest-of-honor on the "tablecloth." It can also be used to create a banner along a wall.

 Shop at dollar stores, flea markets, and garage sales throughout the year and you'll be surprised how many things you'll find that can be used for your next party, not only as decorations and serving containers, but as party favors.

- **Tulle Netting:** Inexpensive white or colored tulle netting is ideal for certain parties, such as an engagement party, anniversary party, bridal shower, wedding rehearsal dinner, or wedding reception. Buy several yards of the least expensive netting you can find, the stiffer the better.
- **Place Cards:** Make your own place cards by cutting 3 1/2 inch squares of heavy paper, using a mat knife. Lightly score the cards in the center, then fold them along the scored crease. Write the guests' names with a fine felt-tip pen and, if appropriate, decorate the place cards with theme-oriented embellishments, such as tiny cloth diapers with gold safety pins for a baby shower; miniature diplomas for a graduation party; or red and pink heart stickers for a Valentine's party.

Small-Budget Party Fun for Children

 typical children's party usually includes some type of favor, goody bags, and one or two games. The trick is to provide this fun on a small budget. Here are inexpensive ideas for all three.

Favors

Theme-related party favors are suggested in chapters throughout this book; however, here are a few affordable all-purpose ideas:

- Stickers
- Erasers
- Wrapped popcorn balls
- Jars of bubbles
- Child's sunglasses
- Instant photo of each guest
- Sidewalk chalk
- Boxes of animal crackers
- Bubble gum
- Coloring books

- Silly string
- Puzzles
- Modeling clay
- Lollipops
- Books of paper dolls
- Jacks
- Kazoos
- Pinwheels
- Crackers (aka "Poppers")

It's easy to make your own crackers. You'll need one toilet paper tube per child, crepe paper, gift-wrap ribbon, and any stickers or decorative touches that complement the party's theme. Cut square pieces of crepe paper 6" longer than the toilet paper tubes. Fill the tubes with candy, confetti, or other surprises, then roll the paper around the tube and tie at each end with ribbons. Cut zigzag edges on each end of the paper. The decorative embellishments can be anything from Santa stickers for a Christmas party, to comic book

Decorate a shoe box, fill with the favors, and place in the center of the table. Tie a piece of crinkle-tie ribbon around each favor with the ends of the ribbons extending to each child's place at the table. At a designated time, let the children pull their ribbons to retrieve their favors.

characters for a Funny Paper Party, to teddy bear stickers for a Teddy Bear Party.

Goody bags

Goody bags (aka "Party Bags," or "Loot Bags," or "Favor Bags") not only add color to children's parties but are also practical because they keep each child's "goodies" in one place. Each bag is filled with such things as candies, favors, or small gifts, depending on the age of the guests. They can range from simple decorated lunch bags to customized containers that complement the party's theme, such as:

- Small metal or paper paint buckets
- Chinese take-out containers
- Burlap sacks tied at the neck with twine
- Mini-pillowcases tied with ribbon
- Large popcorn boxes
- Large drink cups with string handles
- Painted cereal boxes, cut in half (add ribbon "handles")
- Clear or colored cellophane sacks, tied at the necks with ribbon
- Green plastic strawberry baskets, woven with ribbon, with pipe cleaner handles
- Tulle net pouches
- Painted egg cartons

Write the children's names on their bags, using a felt-tip marker or alphabet stickers. By the way, we don't want the birthday child to feel left out, so be sure to provide a goody bag for her as well.

Decorate the containers using broad felt-tip colored markers, wall paper, fabric, or theme-oriented stickers, such as rainbows, such as cartoon characters for a Funny Paper Party.

Games

Obstacle Course Relay Race

Enlist the help of your spouse or a friend to design an obstacle course in your backyard. The course should have a starting point and a finish line, with a dozen or so obstacles in between. Obstacles can include:

- Old tires to hop in and out of.
- A long plastic tube to squiggle through.
- A wading pool to walk through barefoot (taking shoes on/off is part of the race).
- A rope to jump rope with while hopping on one foot.
- A large trash bag, stuffed with crushed newspapers, to jump over.
- A croquet ball to knock through a wicket.
- Monkey bars to swing across.
- A Frisbee flying disc to balance on the child's head while running a certain distance.
- A narrow plank, about a foot off the ground, to walk across.

Divide the players into two or three teams. One team at a time sends a player through the course. As soon as the player has finished, he or she tags the next team member, who then traverses the course. Continue in this way until all the team members have participated. Record the time it takes for each team to run the course. The team with the shortest time wins.

Tennis Ball Baseball

Choose two teams and play regulation baseball, except that instead of batting a baseball, the batter hits a pitched tennis ball with a tennis racket. Once the tennis ball has been hit, the game proceeds as in regular baseball, with players catching or throwing the tennis ball to the bases, and so on.

Tug o' War

Choose two teams and place one group at each end of a husky rope about 100 feet long. Tie a bright ribbon at the middle of the rope. At a signal the teams begin to pull. The object is to pull the opposing team completely over to its side.

Shoelace Hop

Divide into teams of three. Each team of three stands side-by-side and connects their shoes with the shoes of the people on each side of them, using their shoelaces. (For those who aren't wearing laced shoes, provide ropes to tie their ankles together.) At the signal, the teams race to the finish line.

Mini-Golf

Create your own golf course on your lawn. "Holes" are created by laying paper cups on their sides and nailing them to the ground. Furnish standard golf clubs or putters, or use brooms or broom handles instead. You can use golf balls, small rubber balls, or ping pong balls. The child with the fewest number of strokes around the course is declared the winner. Note: The competition can be a simple putting contest using a synthetic indoor putting green.

Flashlight Tag

This version of hide-and-seek is played in the dark. The children run and hide, and the person who's "it" looks for them with a flashlight. Each child who is "tagged" by the flashlight's beam is out. The game continues until the last child is found; that child becomes "it" for the next round.

Black Wolf

This is another version of hide-and-seek that also needs to be played in the dark. One child is the "Black Wolf," and the rest of the children are the "sheep." The object of the game is for the Black Wolf to sneak up on the sheep and, one at a time, drag the sheep back to its den. Once the sheep is in the Wolf's den, however, he can escape if another sheep runs over and touches him before being caught by the Black Wolf. The Black Wolf tries to stay hidden as much as possible so he can sneak up on the sheep, capture one and bring it to his den. The sheep hide from the Black Wolf, but if they see him sneaking up on them, they cry out, "Black Wolf Black Wolf." The children take turns being the Black Wolf.

Burlap Sack Race

Provide one burlap sack for each contestant. Holding the sides of the sack with her hands, each contestant must run or jump her way to the finish line. (Falling down does not disqualify a contestant.) The contestant who reaches the finish line first is declared the winner.

Broom and Hat Race

Divide the children into two teams; supply each team with a broom and a cowboy hat. The child at the front of each line passes the hat on the bristle end of the broom to the next child in line. That child passes it on down and so forth. The first team to pass the hat to the end of the line without dropping it is the winner. If the hat does fall off during the relay, the broom and hat must be brought back to the first person in line, who starts again.

Pin the Tail on the Donkey

We all know how this game is played. You can purchase a Pin the Tail on the Donkey game, or you can create your own by drawing a donkey (or any other animal, such as a cow, cat, or pig) on a large piece of butcher paper and tacking it up on a wall. Blindfold the children one by one and ask them to pin (or tape) the tail on the donkey (or any other animal used for the game). Another variation of this game is to tack up a dozen or so small inflated balloons and have the blindfolded children try to pop them with a pin.

Musical Clothes Bag

A few weeks before the party, begin assembling a trash bag full of silly clothes, boots, scarves, coats, hats, clown noses, novelty nightshirts, ski goggles, and so on. Arrange the children in a circle around the trash bag. Hand an apple to one of the children and have music begin to play. As the music plays, the children must pass the apple around the circle as fast as they can. When the music stops, the child caught holding the apple must go to the trash bag, close his eyes, pull something out, and put it on. Start the music again and let the game continue until the trash bag is empty.

Barber Shop

Divide the guests into teams of two. Each team consists of one barber and one customer. Each barber is given a shaving mug filled with foamy soap, a brush, and a "razor." (Use a rubber knife, tongue depressor, or child's toy razor.) When you say, "Go," each barber ties an apron around the neck of his customer, lathers up his face and gives him a "shave." The judge watches each team to be sure each customer's face is thoroughly lathered and "shaved" without allowing lather to drop onto the floor or the apron. The barber who has shaved his customer the best in the least time wins.

Simon Says

Line the children up in a row facing you. Then give the children instructions, such as "Simon says touch your nose," or "Simon says hop on your right foot," and so on. The gimmick, of course, is to throw in a command that is *not* prefaced by "Simon says." For example, you may say, "Touch your toes." Any child who does so is out of the game because the command was *not* preceded by the magic words, "Simon says." The object of the game is to mix up your commands, which will drop one or two children out of the game every time you omit "Simon says," until only one child—the winner—is left.

Mummy Wrap

Divide the group into two teams. One member of each team volunteers to be the "Mummy." Furnish each team with a large roll of toilet paper and a roll of cellophane tape. When you say "Go," team members begin to wrap their mummies in toilet paper, leaving small holes for the eyes, nose, and mouth. (If a piece of toilet paper breaks off, they must tape it back together.) The first team to use up the roll of toilet paper wins.

Sweat Suit Stuff

Divide the guests into two teams. Ask each team to choose its shortest member to wear extra-large sweatpants and a sweatshirt over his clothes. Furnish each team with 40 small inflated balloons. At the signal, see which team can stuff the most balloons inside the sweatsuit without breaking them. Call time at the end of two minutes.

Orange-Under-the-Chin Race

Divide the guests into two teams. Ask each team to line up in a straight line. Give one orange to each team leader. The goal is to see which team can pass its orange down the line the fastest without dropping it. If a team member drops the orange, the team must start again.

Musical Chairs

Place one chair per child in a circle, with the seats facing out. Have the children stand in front of their respective chairs; play music and have them march around the circle. While the music is playing, remove one chair. When the music stops, the children scramble to find a chair to sit in but, of course, one child will be eliminated each round until there are only two contestants and one chair left. The child who lands in that last chair is declared the winner. To prevent any hard feelings among younger children, it's nice to present each child with a small wrapped gift as he is eliminated from the game. Another way to prevent hard feelings is to have an equal number of chairs as there are participants. One of the chairs is designated as the "King of the Hill." That way, every time the music stops, one child gets to be in the special chair.

Mystery Socks

Fill a dozen or so socks with a variety of items that have identifiable shapes, such as a clothespin, fork, yo-yo, and so on. Provide each child with a piece of paper and a pencil, then arrange the children in a circle. Ask the children to identify the items by feeling them through the socks and writing down what they think they are. When each child has had a turn to feel all the socks and write down her guesses, empty the socks onto the floor. The child with the most correct answers wins.

Ping Pong Ball Hunt

Upon arrival, give each guest a ping pong ball with his or her name on it. Ask the guests to hide the ball very well anywhere in the house (or the yard, or within a certain room, etc.) When the last guest has arrived and hidden a ball, send all the children on a Ping Pong Ball Hunt. The winner is the child whose ball is hidden the best—the last ball to be found.

Musical Statues

Assemble the children in a circle. Whenever the music plays, the children are to dance around the circle, freezing in place whenever the music stops. Don't start the music again until *someone* moves (even blinking or smiling counts!) Believe me, it won't take long! Whoever moves is out of the game. Continue until only one child is left and declared the winner.

Try to Remember

Place several items on a tray, such as a can of dog food, hairbrush, spoon, baseball, or action figure. The older the children, the more items on the tray. Ask the children to look at the items and try to remember them. Then remove the tray from the room. Have the children write down the items from memory. The child with the most correct answers is the winner.

Silly Photo Opps

Create a "photo studio" out of a cardboard refrigerator box. Let each child choose items from a basket filled with funny hats, sunglasses, masks, and humorous clothing from your closet or the thrift shop, such as oversized jackets, evening gowns, scarves, costume jewelry, and so forth. Take instant photos of the guests and display them during the party by using clothespins to hang them from a clothesline that has been suspended across the room. Present the photos to the guests at the end of the party to take home as party favors.

Small-Budget Party Fun for Teens and Adults

Here are popular ways to entertain your guests, all of which require little if any expense, including:

- Musical entertainment
- "This is Your Life" skit
- A "Roast"
- Videotaping the party
- Games

Musical entertainment

Amateur DJ or Recorded Music

If your party theme lends itself to dancing, you might find hidden talent within your family: an aspiring DJ. Put him to work with a selection of tapes and CDs you have chosen ahead of time. Depending on your guests' ages and musical tastes, you can provide anything from country-western line dancing to *slooooow* dancing.

Amateur Talent

Are any of your friends or family members talented amateur musicians? Maybe you have an uncle who does a little piano bar, or perhaps, with a little practice, a singer or group could lip-sync to a recorded hit? Use your imagination and you can provide a lot of fun on a "zero entertainment budget."

"This Is Your Life" Skit

You all remember the old television show, *This Is Your Life*. Well, although the show hasn't been on the air for years, the idea still works today. Nothing is more fun than surprising your guest-of-honor with an overview of his or her life, with mystery guests and surprise guests as well. Putting one of these surprises together takes a lot of work. You'll need to interview the honoree's closest friends and family members, along with people from the past who may be able to attend the party.

Here's a sample "This Is Your Life" scenario to give you an of idea how it works. You'll need to personalize your presentation to coincide with your honoree's life.

Cast:

Master of Ceremonies.
The Guest of Honor.
The Mystery Guests Who Help Tell Her Story.

Set:

A special chair for the guest of honor.

Props:

A large scrapbook that has "This Is Your Life [NAME]" on the front cover.

The show begins:

Master of Ceremonies [as he or she approaches the guest of honor]:
"Are you having a nice time at your party?"
[*The guest-of-honor will undoubtedly answer yes.*]
"Well, it's wonderful to be honored this way by your friends and family, but we have an even bigger surprise for you: [NAME], this is your life!"
[*He shows her the front of the book.*]
[*The honored guest is escorted to her chair of honor.*]

Master of Ceremonies:
"It all began in _____[name of the city and state where the guest-of-honor was born]."

"Mystery" Voice from Offstage:
"I remember it well—I almost didn't make it to the hospital in time."

[*And out comes her mother, of course, who hugs her daughter and continues with any humorous or interesting facts relating to her daughter's birth.*]

Other Voices from Offstage:
- An aunt or other relative who tells a story about something funny the guest-of-honor did when she was a little girl, or what she liked to eat, or how she found a kitten and brought it home, and so on.
- Her sister, who tells what she was like as a teenager and how she always got into her lipstick, borrowed her clothes, and so on.
- Her best friend, who tells about the time they got lost in a snowstorm because she was too stubborn to stop and ask for directions, and so on.
- Her high school drama teacher, who tells about the time she had the lead in the senior play.
- The honored guest's grandmother (or some other friend or relative who traveled a long distance to surprise her by being at the party), who tells how proud she was of her on the day she graduated from high school, or college, or another important event.

The "mystery guests" should appear in chronological order, corresponding with the events in the honored guest's life. For example, someone may tell about how sweet or ornery she was as a toddler; then the next person may tell about how she led her team to the state softball championship in high school; and so forth.

The last guest is the honored guest's boyfriend, fiancé, or spouse (who has been hidden away in a back bedroom all this time.) Of course, his appearance is the best surprise of all and brings her story to an end.

If you can pull this off, and it's really a surprise, the party will be a guaranteed success!

A "Roast"

The idea of a "roast" is to take turns making jokes and telling embarrassing little stories about the guest-of-honor, but only in fun, never revealing anything too personal or humiliating.

For example, the honored guest's best friend might tell about the time she unknowingly stepped in a "doggie gift" on her way to speak at a women's luncheon and how the stench permeated the room throughout her speech. Or, Dad might tell about the time he was teaching his son to drive and some of the klutzy things his son did.

A successful roast depends on how well you've done your research and how well-prepared the guests are to tell their *harmless* stories.

Videotape the party

If you can get hold of a video camera and a videotape, you'll have winning entertainment near the end of your party, because *everyone* loves to see how he or she looks on video. If you can catch one of the guests acting up or in an embarrassing moment, so much the better. The trick is to videotape interesting things that happen during the party, from each guest's arrival at the door, to the hostess stirring the fudge sauce in the kitchen, to "Mr. Personality" who gets carried away with a fish story, or how his car broke down, and so forth.

In the case of an engagement party, wedding rehearsal dinner party, or an anniversary party, personal interviews work well. Ask each guest how he or she met the couple, the funniest thing that happened when they were in college together, or the cutest or naughtiest thing he or she did as a child, and so forth. Play the videotape at the end of the party, then present the tape to the guest(s) of honor as a memento of the party.

Tips on Videotaping a Party:

- Get plenty of close-ups.
- Don't swing the camera around the room. Keep it steady as you tape or you'll make the guests "seasick" when they watch the video later on.
- Assign the job to someone who will enjoy the task. Don't try to combine the videotaping responsibility with playing host or hostess.

Games

If you decide to play a game or two at your party, keep several things in mind: the formality of your party; the theme of your party; and the ages of your guests. The idea is to choose games and activities that will come as close as possible to pleasing everyone.

Who Am I?

This is a great get-acquainted game because it forces the guests to talk to each other. Cut paper into pieces approximately 3 by 5 inches, then write the name of a famous person on each. Pin one of these cards to each guest's back. Each person can see the names on the backs of the other guests, but can't, of course, see his own. The idea of the game is for a player to determine whose name is pinned on his back by asking questions about that person.

As the game begins, each player is allowed to ask three questions per round that can be answered only with a yes or no, such as, "Am I living?" "Am I a female?" "Am I an American?"

The first player to guess the name on his back is declared the winner.

Charades

Charades is probably the most popular party game in America today. Divide the guests into two teams—evenly divided or the men against the women, older generation against younger generation, and so forth. Each team comes up with the titles of six or eight books, movies, television shows, or songs. They write the titles on pieces of paper, which are folded and placed in a basket. The teams take turns drawing a piece of paper from the opposing team's basket, although the only person who sees the title is the person who will be acting it out.

A timer is set and this person has three minutes to silently act out the title, using his hands, body, and facial expressions to communicate the title to his team. If the timer rings before the team has guessed the title, the opposing team gets five points. If the team guesses the title before the timer expires, it gets ten points. After each side has had six or eight turns, the team with the most points wins. In the case of a tie, play one more round.

Another version of this game is to draw the clues, instead of act them out, resulting in a game similar to Pictionary.

Note: Not everyone is comfortable "acting out" in front of a group, so it's a good idea to have less turns per side than there are team members. This means that certain team members can decline graciously without feeling pressured.

The Newlywed/Oldywed Game

We all know how the Newlywed Game is played, and it works for "Oldyweds" as well. Four couples are chosen to compete. The men leave the room and the women are asked questions, which are recorded. The men come back into the room and are asked the same questions. The object is for the men to respond with the same answers as their partners. Then, the game is reversed and the women leave the room as the men are asked questions, and so forth. The couple with the most matching answers wins.

Here are some typical questions:

- Who is his favorite professional sports hero?
- Who is her favorite male movie star?
- When was your last fight?
- When was the last time she burned the dinner?
- What is the most embarrassing thing that ever happened to him?
- What is her most obnoxious habit?
- What turns him off about a woman?

Masquerade Race

This is a lot of fun for a couples' party, a competition between the men and the women. Assemble two huge shopping bags full of clothes ahead of time, one filled with men's clothes, such as pants, belt, long sleeved shirt, tie, hat, and gloves, and the other with women's clothes, such as a *large* dress or housecoat, belt, jewelry, scarf, hat, socks, and slippers.

The men "volunteer" one of their own to be "it" and the women do the same.

At a given signal, the man and woman turn their backs to the guests and get dressed (over their own clothes) as fast as they can, the man donning the woman's clothes and the woman the man's. The first one completely finished wins (all zippers must be zipped; all buttons buttoned; the tie tied correctly, and so forth).

The Dictionary Game

Assemble:
- A dictionary.
- Several pads of note paper.
- One pen per person.

The idea of this game is to choose an unusual word from the dictionary, hopefully one that is unfamiliar to the players.

Round One:

- Step I: A person is chosen to be the leader of Round One; he announces the word he has chosen to the group. If anyone knows the meaning of the word, the word is disqualified and another must be selected.
- Step II: The leader writes the *true* dictionary definition of the word on a piece of paper.
- Step III: The remaining players write down *fictional* definitions that are as believable as possible.
- Step IV – All pieces of paper are turned in to the leader who reads each definition out loud, maintaining as straight a face as possible.
- Step V – Each player announces which definition he believes to be true.
- Step VI – Each player who chooses the correct definition receives one point. Each player whose false definition was chosen by another player receives one point. The leader receives five points if *no one* chose the correct dictionary definition.

This is the end of Round One. Play continues as another player is chosen to be the leader, and so on until everyone has had a turn. The winner is the player with the most total points at the end of all the rounds.

Clothespin Game

Purchase a supply of colorful plastic clothespins. Pin one clothespin on each guest's clothing and let the game begin. Set a timer for 20 minutes. During that 20-minute period no one is allowed to say the word *no*. So, the idea of the game is to ask the guests questions about themselves, baiting them to answer no. Any guest who does must relinquish his clothespin to the person who tricked him into saying the forbidden word. When the timer rings, the guest with the most clothespins wins.

A variation of this game, by the way, especially popular at bridal showers, is played throughout the party. The guests are told their clothespins will be taken away by whoever catches them crossing their legs. The guest who has caught the most women crossing their legs during the party wins.

The Observation Game

Arrange 15 or 20 items on a tray, such as a pocket knife, a pencil, a fork, and so forth. Then ask a friend or your co-host to walk slowly around the room, displaying the tray for all the guests to see.

Everyone is given paper and pencil, and as soon as your friend has left the room with the tray, the guests will be asked to write down as many things as they can remember about *your friend* (color of hair and eyes; what she was wearing; and so on)!

The guests will moan and cry foul, of course, but they'll finally settle down and start recording things they remember about your friend. The guest who has recorded the most accurate description wins a prize.

Identification Game

This is a humorous couples' contest. String a few sheets on a clothes-line across the room. Have the men stand behind the sheets, exposing their bare legs and feet from the knees down. Then have each woman try to identify her man's legs, at which time she stands in front of the sheet at that spot.

Then, the sheets are removed and prizes go to those women who were right. (You'll be surprised how many women can't identify their partners' legs and feet in a game like this!)

There are several fun variations to this game as well. For example, you can cut holes in the sheets and have the men try to identify the women's eyes, or have the women try to choose which noses belong to their partners. (This is my favorite because there's nothing quite so funny as a row of noses poking through the holes in the sheet!)

Another variation, although I don't think the men appreciate it, is for the women to identify their men's pates. The men line up behind the sheet and turn their backs so that only the tops of their heads are showing. (Nothing below the ears should be visible.)

Mad Hatter Contest

Ask your guests to wear "mad hats" to the party. Any type of hat will do, but the key is to embellish it to the hilt, with prizes given for "Most Outrageous," "Most Creative," "Silliest," and so forth.

Door Prize Gimmicks

Guests love the idea of door prizes, which may be something inex-pensive you've purchased and wrapped ahead of time or part of your

- If you're looking for specific wedding shower games or baby shower games, you'll find them in my books *Complete Book of Wedding Showers* and *Complete Book of Baby Showers*. I also include a few in Chapters 30 and 33 of this book.
- You will find theme-related games and entertainment in many of the specific theme parties described in the rest of the book.

decorations, such as table centerpieces, potted plants, or floral arrangements. Here are a few of the most popular ways to determine who wins a door prize:

- Number the backs of the name tags before they are given to the guests as they arrive, beginning with the number "1." Then, place corresponding numbers on pieces of paper that are wadded up and placed in a basket. Near the end of the party, ask the guest-of-honor to draw a wad of paper out of the basket. The winning number receives the prize.

- A variation of this is to insert three wads of paper (with pre-determined numbers) inside three balloons *before* they are blown up. Arrange the balloons in a bouquet as part of the decorations. Then, near the end of the party, ask the guest-of-honor to select one of the balloons and burst it by sitting on it (no hands allowed!) The wad of paper is then unfolded and the number read. The person with the corresponding number on the back of her name tag wins a door prizes. Repeat this same procedure for the second and third balloons.

- If the party is a sit-down meal, place a sticker under the seats of two or three of the dining room chairs. After dessert has been served, ask the guests to look under their chairs to see who has the stickers. Those who do win prizes.

- Let the guests guess how many chocolate kisses, candy hearts, or roasted almonds there are in a large, clear glass jar. The guest who comes closest to the correct answer wins the jar full of goodies.

Small-Budget Birthday Parties

This section features small-budget birthday parties with specific themes, coordinated to include affordable invitations, costumes, decorations, party fun, and party fare. Each party carries a specific theme from beginning to end, so everything is there for you and—best of all—everything you need to pull it off is either free or very inexpensive.

Oh, joy! Awesome parties on a budget, exactly what we need these days.

Baby's First Birthday Party

If this is your baby's first birthday party and you're trying to keep the costs down, you're in luck because a 1-year-old child is very easy to please! You see, the reason baby's first party often costs more than it should is because of *adult expectations*, not the *baby's*!

Your baby may be the youngest of a large family where Grandma, Grandpa, Auntie Louise, and Uncle Joseph expect a grand affair, and if this is the case, let *them* play hosts. Otherwise, plan an economical party your baby will love by simply splashing the party venue with bright colors.

Invitations

- Buy a package of small, colorful balloons. Use these balloons as your invitations. Blow up the balloons, tie with crinkle-tie ribbon, print the invitation on each balloon with a black felt-tip marker, then hand-deliver or deflate and mail to the parents of the children being invited to the party.

Decorations

- Decorate with brightly colored balloons; they don't have to be helium-filled. They can be hung by crinkle-tie ribbon from doorways or chandeliers, and they can be set in cereal-sized bowls around the table top.
- Spread your table with a colorful tablecloth and napkins, or a brightly colored twin-sized sheet. You don't need to purchase paper tablecloth and napkins.

- Colorful crepe paper streamers or crinkle-tie ribbons can be "curled" and hung around the party venue.

Fun stuff

- Play balloon volleyball by bopping a balloon back and forth over a table or chair.
- Play Musical Party Hat, a variation of Musical Chairs, where one hat is passed around the table from head to head while the music plays. When the music stops, one of the guests will be wearing the hat. The music resumes and the hat continues around the table until it finally lands on the birthday boy or girl. At that point each of the guests is given a party hat to wear for the rest of the party. (This game requires the help of a few adults or teens.)

Be flexible! If the birthday boy falls asleep during the party, that's okay! Or, if he throws his party hat on the floor, what difference does it really make? Absolutely none!

Party fare

- Serve baby-sized finger foods, such as Jell-O Jigglers (see Chapter 43) and peanut butter and jelly sandwiches cut into animal shapes with a cookie cutter.
- Birthday cake and ice cream are the highlights of this party, so light that candle and take photos galore!

Teddy Bear Party (Ages 2-7)

T his is a favorite party theme for the younger set, and it can definitely be hosted on a small budget. Not only do you decorate the room and serving table with stuffed bears, but you ask each child to bring his or her own personal teddy bear as a "guest" to the party, which provides free ambience and decorations for your party.

Invitations

Make bear invitations out of brown construction paper. The first step is to make a pattern out of heavy paper cut into a 4-inch square. Draw eight circles: a large center circle (the bear's tummy), four smaller circles (the bear's paws), one medium-sized circle (the bear's head), and two small half-circle ears. Cut around the outside of the circles you have drawn and you will have a pattern for your bear invitations. The next step is to trace this pattern onto brown construction paper. Cut pieces 4 inches wide by 8 inches long. Fold each piece in half long ways, which will result in a piece 4 inches square (folded at the top). Use a black felt-tip marker to draw a face on each bear, then write, "You're invited to a Teddy Bear Party" on the front, and the details of the party on the inside of each invitation. Be sure to ask the children to bring their own personal teddy bears as guests to the party. These invitations may be sent through the mail or hand-delivered to save postage.

Decorations

- Greet the children at the front door with a "stuffed bear" sitting in a lawn chair (made of a pair of overalls, shirt, tie, boots, all stuffed with wadded-up newspaper, with the head of a real teddy bear sticking out from the shirt's collar.)

- Round up all the teddy bears you can find, tie ribbons around their necks, place party hats on their heads and tie balloons around their wrists. Set them around the room—sitting in a rocking chair, peeking out from behind a sofa, or clustered together as a table centerpiece.

Fun stuff

- Teddy Bear Hats: Provide several colors of construction paper or light poster board, stickers, crayons, felt-tip markers, scissors, and glue. Help the children cut out "crowns" or hats, one for each child and one for the bear the child brought to the party.
- Pass the Teddy: Divide the children into two teams. The first child in each line must put a teddy bear (the bigger the better) under his or her chin and pass it to the next child in line, who grabs it with his or her chin, and so forth, until it arrives at the end of the line. If the teddy bear is dropped, the team must start again. The first team to pass the teddy from the front to the back of the line without dropping it wins.
- Play "Musical Teddies": This is traditional musical chairs (see Chapter 3), except that instead of the children sitting in the chairs, they place their teddies in the chairs instead.

Party Fare

- Serve Teddy Bear cookies (made from sugar cookie dough).
- Decorate the birthday cake with miniature teddy bears sitting with "gifts" in their laps (tiny gift-wrapped "boxes" made by gift-wrapping sugar cubes.)

Prizes/Favors

The children may take home their Teddy Bear Hats as party favors, or you may be able to find inexpensive Goldilocks and the Three Bears coloring books that may be used as prizes or favors.

Peeper Family Puppet Party (Ages 3-7)

Here's a fun, economical party theme for the younger crowd. Use empty square tissue boxes and inexpensive cloth garden gloves or plastic gloves to create a puppet family that pops up and "peeps" out the top of its "house." The house, of course, is a decorated square tissue box.

Invitations

Make your own invitations by tracing your child's hand on the fronts of folded 8-1/2 x 11 inch pieces of brightly colored construction paper. Use felt-tip pens to draw little puppet faces on the end of each finger. Hand-print the invitation on the inside of each piece of paper; send through the mail, fax, or hand-deliver.

Decorations

Decorate the room with large stuffed brown grocery sacks or white plastic trash bags fashioned into "puppets." Convert the sacks into colorful puppets by creating faces, hair, collars, bow ties, buttons, and clothes out of yarn, ribbon, fabric scraps, bright construction paper, wrapping paper, old greeting cards, empty spools of thread, and so forth. Use a hot glue gun or ordinary household glue to attach the items to the sacks. Be as creative and colorful as possible. Use these sack puppets to decorate the walls, ceiling, and serving table.

Fun stuff

- The highlight of this Peeper Family Puppet Party is having the children create finger puppets that live in empty tissue boxes, decorated to resemble Peeper Family houses (puppet stages.) A round hole needs to be cut out of the bottom of each "house," big enough for a child to insert his glove puppet. Provide each child with a single white cloth garden glove or plastic glove, available from your local hardware store. Protect your table with a large sheet of plastic, then let the children paint the "houses" with poster paint and create finger puppets by converting each finger on the gloves into members of the Peeper Family: Daddy Peeper, Mommy Peeper, Brother Peeper, Sister Peeper, and Baby Peeper.

Hair: Small pompoms or pieces of yarn.
Eyes: Draw on with magic markers or supply wiggly eyes that can be attached with craft glue or a hot glue gun.
Facial features: Draw on the rest of the facial features (smiley mouths, noses, rosy cheeks, freckles, eyebrows, and so forth) with felt markers.
Clothes: Cut miniature collars, hats, jackets, skirts, and pants out of felt or scrap fabric and glue to each finger puppet.
Accessories: Tie narrow ribbons around the puppets' necks and add tiny buttons to jackets or sequins as earrings, necklaces, fancy buttons, or adornments for the puppets' hats.

• Once all the children have finished making their houses and glove puppets, ask each child to insert his hand through the bottom of his house, extending his hand through the hole on top, just far enough for the fingers of the glove to be seen. Then the children make up their own puppet dialogue or puppet songs as the finger puppets talk and sing to each other. Children love make-believe, especially in this age group, so they will invent their own fun as the puppets carry on their conversations.

• Each child is provided with a lollipop to be decorated as a "puppet on a stick." Depending on your budget, you can buy a sack of Tootsie Pops or generic safety pops that can be divided among the children, or you may be able to find larger-sized lollipops on sale; give one per child. Provide tubes of frosting to decorate the lollipops, adding eyes, nose, mouth, ears, hair, and so forth. Tie each lollipop "puppet" with a ribbon under its "chin." This project will amuse the kids for 15 minutes or so. The lollipop puppets may then be eaten as party snacks, or they may be taken home as party favors.

- Allow plenty of time for the children to convert the tissue boxes into houses and the gloves into finger puppets. They'll get caught up in the fun, but you'll need a few teenagers or adults to help the children with the cutting, gluing, and painting.
- Have the children's puppets sing "Happy Birthday" to the guest-of-honor.

Party Fare

Serve a cake decorated with your own garden glove that has been converted to members of the Peeper Family; the glove lies flat on the cake.

Prizes/Favors

Each child takes home his "Peeper Puppet Family" glove and "Peeper Family Home" as party favors.

The Big Race (Ages 4-7)

Here's a clever theme for a small party budget. It involves a little work ahead of time because you'll need to scour your community for large cardboard boxes, one per child. The boxes are converted into race cars during the party.

The boxes should be appliance sized, such as dishwasher, TV, or microwave boxes. Or, if you know of a family who has just moved into a home and has oversized packing boxes left over, these will work as well.

Invitations

A month or so before the party, convert one of these boxes into a race car (see "Fun Stuff," on page 52 for instructions). Then, take a photo of your birthday child in the race car. Make copies on your computer scanner or at your local copy store, placing the photo so that it prints out on the bottom half of each copy. Fold each copy in half, print the invitation on the inside, and hand-deliver or fax to the guests. Ask the children to wear their bicycle or skateboarding helmets and safety or ski goggles to the party.

Decorations

- Decorate a Race Track Cake with an oval track and miniature race cars. Cover the cake with brown frosting and draw the track with a tube of white frosting. Add crossed black-and-white checkered flags at the finish line (use black felt-tip marker to draw squares on small white paper flags).

- Suspend black and white twisted crepe paper streamers from the ceiling over the center of the serving table, attaching the ends to the corners of the table, creating a canopy.
- Decorate the walls with racing posters or large black-and-white checkered flags.
- Make a gas station pump out of a tall cardboard box, or stack several smaller boxes. Paint the boxes with tempura paint, then use a wide black felt-tip marker to print the price per gallon, total number of gallons, and so on at the top of the pump.

 **A tip.**   Allow plenty of time for the children to build their cars. The race itself won't take long at all.

Fun stuff

- Provide each child with a cardboard box, along with stickers, broad felt-tip markers, large crayons, and accessories, such as tires and steering wheels (colored plastic plates), headlights (small aluminum pie plates), and windshield wipers (disposable chop sticks). Finally, the children add racing stripes (brightly colored plastic tape), numbers, their names, and sponsor's logos, such as a cat's face for Wild Cat Motor Oil, and so forth. Use packing tape, a hot glue gun, and a staple gun to help the children attach their accessories.
- When the children have finished building their cars, they don their helmets and goggles, climb in (stand inside their boxes, holding onto the sides), and race around the block. Use checkered flags to declare the winner(s) and hand out prizes to all the children, whether they won or not.
- Videotape all the activities, including building the race cars and the big race itself. Show the tape as the children eat their cake and ice cream.

Party Fare

- Serve the cake described earlier, along with your child's favorite ice cream.

Prizes/Favors

- Send the children home with their race cars, along with instant photos of each child in his car.

Let's Play Dress-Up (Ages 4-11)

Here's an economical party theme that children love: "Let's Play Dress-Up." Kids like to pretend they are grownups, of course, but they also like to dress up as cowboys, astronauts, hula dancers, the Karate Kid or any of their movie or video game heroes.

Invitations

Purchase an inexpensive book of paper dolls; punch out the "clothes" and print the invitation on the back of each "outfit." Insert the outfits into legal-sized envelopes and mail or hand-deliver.

Costumes

- As hostess, you should wear a humorous outfit of some type, such as an evening gown, embellished with costume jewelry and a sparkly crown.
- The children will soon join you once they are all dressed up in their favorite outfits.

Decorations

- Decorate with clothes racks full of dress-up clothes, plus baskets filled with hats, shoes, canes, umbrellas, shawls, scarves, wigs, ties, helmets, swords, bride's veils, capes, purses, and so on. (Raid your local Goodwill or thrift shop, plus you can ask the parents to contribute to the cause. Be sure the clothes and accessories are identified with tags or markings so they can be returned after the party.)

- Decorate the serving table with dolls that are all dressed up (add a few extras, such as strings of sequins for Barbie and a tall black top hat for Ken.)
- Provide one or two floor-length mirrors decorated with balloons and streamers.

Fun stuff

- The fun of this party is to play dress-up. To prolong the fun, take instant photos of each child in his or her outfit, but encourage the children to switch clothes so that each child has at least three "photo opps." Send the photos home with the children as party favors.
- Provide "stations" manned by four of your friends who have agreed to serve as makeup artist, manicurist, hair stylist, and jewelry coordinator. Round up plenty of costume jewelry, makeup, nail polish, and fake nails, plus hot rollers and hair spray for exotic "makeovers." The children will line up at each station, anxious to receive their mustaches, beards, long, decorated fingernails, glittery "up-dos," glamorous jewelry, and so on.
- To top it all off, walk around the room and spray the girls with perfume or cologne and splash a little after-shave on the boys.
- Videotape the activities and play the tape back near the end of the party so the children can see themselves in their outfits.

A tip.

One of my friends hosted a party for 5th grade girls where they "modeled" her negligees and baby doll pajamas. She said it was the easiest party to plan because all she had to do was empty her dresser drawers. She "made up" the girls from her own makeup supplies.

Party Fare

- Serve "grownup" party foods on "grownup" serving platters, such as fancy appetizers, and serve ginger ale in long-stemmed, plastic champagne glasses.
- Decorate the birthday cake with paper dolls and their "clothes."

Prizes/Favors

Send the children home with their instant photos.

Petting Zoo Party (Ages 4-12)

This party requires live animals, so you'll need to borrow them, "rent" them, or have the guests bring their own. The pets can be anything from gold fish to turtles to full-sized horses—the more, the better! This is another case of an affordable party theme where the pets "decorate" the party venue at no expense to you.

Invitations

Purchase a box of inexpensive dog biscuits. Computer-generate or make your own hand-printed invitations; attach one to each dog biscuit and hand-deliver. Ask the guests to dress casually and to bring their pets to the party. (Be sure to have them bring their own leashes, cages, water bowls, and food, if necessary.)

Decorations

- You can decorate with posters of animals, a decorated dog house, sacks of animal food, or oversized baby bottles, which can be purchased from a veterinary supply store.
- Make animal cages out of cardboard boxes: Cut open one side of the box and make bars using black crepe paper strips. Place stuffed animals inside the boxes.

Fun Stuff

- Most of the time is spent petting the animals, riding the animals, if appropriate, and taking instant photos of the guests with their pets; the photos are sent home as party favors.

59

- Ask your local pet store owner to provide a variety of pets for the party, such as puppies, kittens, or talking parrots.
- If appropriate, have a "fetching" contest or Frisbee toss for the dogs attending the party. Award prizes to the dogs' owners.
- Have the children dress up their pets for the party. Provide a supply of tulle netting (for tutus), ribbons, birthday hats, sunglasses, glittery crowns, and colorful fabrics (to make "shirts," "skirts," "shorts", and so on.) Award prizes for the various categories, such as "Funniest," "Most Creative," and "Cutest.".
- Video tape the party from beginning to end. Show the tape near the end of the party while the kids are eating their cake and ice cream and the birthday child is opening gifts.

 To save money on tulle netting, ribbons, and other pet accessories, ask the guests to bring their pets already dressed up for the party.

Party Fare

Decorate the birthday cake with tiny stuffed animals on leashes. Serve with ice cream in clean plastic dog dishes.

Prizes/Favors

Send guests home with instant photos of them with their pets.

Outer Space Party (Ages 5-9)

Y ou may call your party an Astronaut Party, Martian Party, *Star Trek* or *Star Wars* Party, depending on the ages of the guests.

Invitations

Hand-deliver "moon rocks" with your handmade invitations. The moon rocks can be created inexpensively by spray painting ordinary rocks with silver paint, then writing "Official Moon Rock" on each with a permanent black marker. Use the same marker to hand-print the invitations, which are attached to the rocks.

Costumes

Any time you can talk guests into wearing costumes, you have added to a party's ambience for free. So, ask your guests to come dressed as their favorite characters: martians, astronauts, or *Star Trek* or *Star Wars* characters.

Decorations

- When you're spray painting the fist-sized "moon rocks" to send with the invitations, spray paint one larger "moon rock" (as large as you can carry) to place on your serving table.
- Drag out your small white Christmas lights and drape the strands from the ceiling, filling the darkened party venue with stars.

- Suspend "planets" from the ceiling as well. They may be ping pong balls, Styrofoam balls, or white tennis balls.
- Instead of a tablecloth, use a sheet of wrinkled heavy-duty aluminum foil on the serving table.

Fun Stuff

- If the party is after dark, borrow a good-quality telescope. Let the children take turns viewing planets, stars, or the moon.
- For the older children, play the "I'm Going to Mars" game. The children sit in a circle and one says, "I'm going to Mars and I'm going to take (any item of the child's choice, such as his pet) with me." The next child repeats what the first child said, adding another item of his own, and so forth around the circle.
- Here's an economical project: Several weeks before the party, start saving everything you can find that can be used for building "spaceships" (foil, empty cans, paper towel and toilet paper tubes, small cereal boxes, empty coffee cans, and so on). Divide the materials you've collected into four piles, along with tape, stapler, scissors, paper clips, felt-tip markers, glue, and construction paper. Assign a group of children to each pile to see which one can build the best spaceship.

Party Fare

- Serve "space food," such as powdered orange drink, dried fruits, beef jerky, and so forth.
- Decorate a cake to resemble the surface of the moon by spreading the white frosting in lumpy, wavy patterns. Set a plastic astronaut and a small United States flag on top of the cake. Surround the cake with more spray-painted "moon rocks."

Drive-In Movie Party (Ages 7-12)

ere's a popular party theme for this age group: a drive-in movie, right in your own backyard. This party takes place outdoors after dark so, for most parts of the country, it needs to be a summer party.

Invitations

Computer-generate or hand-draw a "movie bill" advertising the video movie that will be shown at your backyard drive-in theater. At the bottom of the page, list the location of the drive-in theater, date and time of showing, and the name of the birthday child.

Decorations

Create an enclosed theater in your backyard by stringing rope from tree to tree to patio posts, and so forth. Then drape the ropes with sheets, quilts, and blankets to enclose the theater. Bring a TV and VCR to the front of the theater for showing the video. Set up chairs facing the TV or throw out sleeping bags or quilts with plenty of pillows for TV watching.

Fun Stuff

- The birthday child opens gifts and the cake and ice cream are served before the video is shown.
- Rent a movie you're sure the children will like and show it in your outdoor "drive-in" theater while the kids flake out on the sleeping bags or sit in the chairs.

63

- Skim through the movie ahead of time and make up a list of trivia questions. Hand them out after the movie and award a prize to the child who has the most correct answers.

A tip. If the temperature may be cooling off before the movie is over, ask the children to wear or bring warm sweatshirts and sweatpants to the party.

Party Fare

- Serve cake and ice cream before the movie. For the cake, use frosting tubes to create a duplicate of the movie bill that was sent out as an invitation.
- Provide movie-watching goodies during the movie: popcorn; inexpensive lemonade drinks made from powdered mix; and candy (look for bargain candies in bulk at your favorite discount store.) Serve the popcorn in white cardboard paint tubs, affordably priced at your discount hardware store.

Funny Paper Party (Ages 8-12)

This party theme is inspired by your Sunday newspaper funny paper section, so start saving now—you'll need a lot of them!

Invitations

Cut poster board into 5 x 7-inch pieces. Fold them in half so they measure 5 x 3-1/2 inches. Cut out characters from the funny papers; glue one on the front of each folded invitation. Draw "speech bubbles" from the mouths of the cartoon characters that say, "Come to My Funny Paper Party." Hand-print the invitation itself inside each folded piece, adding this: "Come dressed as your favorite funny paper character." Mail or hand-deliver.

Costumes

Everyone should be dressed as a funny paper character, including the birthday child and you as host or hostess. Suggestions: Mickey Mouse, Minnie Mouse, Bugs Bunny, Goofy, Charlie Brown, Lucy, Archie, Bart Simpson, Porky Pig, Sylvester the Cat, Dilbert, Snoopy, and so forth.

Decorations

Talk about "affordable," the decorations for this party are made from funny papers and comic books. Tape funny paper pages together to make a tablecloth; fold pages into three-cornered birthday hats; hang pages on the walls; purchase inexpensive cardboard paint tubs from your discount hardware store and decorate them with funny paper characters; line the paint tubs with more funny paper pages (in lieu of tissue paper) to use as "goody buckets" for each child. Tear out sheets from comic books and use them as place mats or to decorate the walls.

 **A tip.** Call the guests' parents ahead of time to remind them their children should come dressed as a funny paper character; have suggestions ready.

Fun Stuff

- Play cartoon videos.
- Play "Who Am I?" using cartoon characters instead of famous persons (see Chapter 4).
- Play "Mickey Says" (same as Simon Says, see Chapter 3).
- Funny Paper Hat Contest: Furnish the children with funny papers, a stapler, tape, silk flowers, buttons, ribbons, and other novelty accessories. Award prizes for "funniest," "most original," and so forth.

Party Fare

- Decorate the cake with an enlarged funny paper character (glued to a piece of poster board) placed on top of white icing. (Enlarge a character at your copy shop or by using your computer scanner.) Use a loop of thin licorice to form a "speech bubble" on the cake that says, "Happy Birthday [NAME] ." Cut strips of poster board to fit the outside edges of the cake; glue comic strips onto the poster board. Serve with Neapolitan ice cream.
- Serve "Charlie Brown's Favorite Bug Punch" (see Chapter 42).

Prizes/Favors

- Comic books.
- Coloring books featuring funny paper characters.
- Cartoon character stickers.

Sweet 16 Party

When a girl reaches her 16th birthday, it's nice to honor her with a special party, called a "Sweet 16 Party." Reaching the age of 16 is considered by many to be the day she reaches womanhood. Most girls prefer an all-girl party, even a slumber party with her favorite girlfriends as guests. Or, the party may be an informal theme-related co-ed party, such as a hayride with a barbecue. A semi-formal co-ed party with dinner and dancing is often co-hosted by the parents, grandparents, aunts, uncles, and other family members. The idea of a semi-formal dinner and dance, by the way, doesn't necessarily have to be an expensive affair. First of all, if it's co-hosted, the total expense of the party is split multiple ways. Or, if you're hosting it yourself, you can still provide an elegant sit-down dinner (see Chapter 44) with music for dancing, using recorded music or an affordable DJ.

Invitations

- An informal all-girl or co-ed party requires nothing more than verbal invitations delivered over the telephone or in person.
- A semi-formal party requires a nicer invitation, which can be created inexpensively by computer-generating the wording, using an elegant italicized font and printing on sheets of white parchment paper. Or, if you don't have access to a computer, you can make a master copy by using black ink and a calligraphy pen, then make copies onto parchment at a copy shop. The invitations will need

to be placed in high-quality envelopes, but they may be hand-delivered to save money on postage.

Decorations

Depending on whether the party is formal or informal, use one or more of the low-budget decorating ideas suggested in Chapter 2. Or, if it's a theme-related party, borrow suggestions from theme parties described in this book. In any case, you *must* provide 16 candles, whether they are tall tapered birthday candles on her cake or sixteen candles mounted in candleholders of various heights. Tie candles at their bases with narrow satin ribbons.

This is one of those parties where it's important to plan the party with the help of your daughter. Don't launch into plans for a dinner-dance if she feels uncomfortable with the co-ed idea, for example.

Fun Stuff

- A semi-formal dinner-dance is easy to plan when it comes to "fun stuff," because the dinner takes up a good part of the evening, followed by dancing to recorded music.
- Of course, singing "Happy Birthday" to the birthday girl and watching her open her gifts is always a highlight of one of these parties.

Party Fare

- See Chapter 44 for formal and informal party fare.
- A cake with 16 candles is a must!

Winter Beach Party (Teen Birthday Party)

Your teenager will love this idea, a great cold-weather birthday party theme, especially in the Northeast and Midwest when temperatures dip below freezing. And best of all, it's another small-budget party theme in which the "costumes" and "decorations" make the party.

Invitations

Computer-generate your invitations, incorporating beach scenes, or create an original master invitation with clip art of beach balls or beach umbrellas, plus models wearing swimsuits. Add the party information, then copy onto colored paper at your local copy store. Optional: Enclose your invitations in sealable sandwich baggies that contain sand and a few small sea shells.

Costumes

Ask the guests to wear their swimsuits, cover-ups, beach shoes, and straw hats, and to bring colorful beach towels.

Decorations

- Decorate the room with "palm trees" cut out of poster board, embellished with green paper fronds. Also, add travel posters of warm beach destinations.
- Borrow beach chairs, colorful beach umbrellas, and plenty of beach towels to spread around the floor.

- Dress any stuffed animal in a swimsuit, straw hat, and sunglasses; place him on a beach towel on one of the beach chairs.
- Decorate the serving table with a sandy beach: Pour sand in a pile on the table, add seashells and a miniature volleyball court. Create the court by drawing the outline with a knife, then suspend a net across the middle of the court. Cut an old hairnet into a volleyball net, attached to poles (wooden matchsticks) that are mounted in one-inch squares of child's modeling clay.

Fun Stuff

Several games from Chapter 4 will work well for one of these parties, such as Charades, plus a hula contest or a hula hoop contest.

 **A tip.**

- Several hours before the party begins, turn the thermostat up to 80 degrees or higher; the house needs to be "toasty warm" in order to pull off this party theme in the winter.
- Play Caribbean or Hawaiian music during the party.
- Borrow surfboards to use as decorations, plus set one on your serving table to use as a "surfboard buffet."

Party Fare

- Serve economical beach party food: roast hot dogs and marshmallows over the fire (use your fireplace); add some "old-fashioned picnic" dishes (see Chapter 23); and serve cold soda from a galvanized tub filled with ice.
- Serve S'Mores, which require roasting marshmallows over the fireplace (see Chapter 43).
- Serve traditional birthday cake with an ocean beach scene, complete with "beach umbrellas," (tiny paper cocktail umbrellas).

Tacky Party
(Teen Party)

his is a tongue-in-cheek party theme that fits perfectly in a small-budget party book, because how costly can it be to host a party where *everything* is deliberately done in a tacky way, from the invitations, to the decorations, to the attire, to the refreshments. This is a chance for everyone to leave their troubles at home, loosen up, and enjoy "acting out."

Invitations

In order to have the proper degree of "tackiness," the invitations need to be hand-crafted. Include misspelled words, small embellishments that have been glued on crooked, plus smudges and torn corners. Mail in old envelopes that have had the old addresses blacked out and new stamps attached. (Be sure to ask the guests to wear the tackiest outfits they can find to the party.)

Costumes

- Hopefully, the guests will be dressed nice and tacky: unlaced combat boots with an evening gown; long white gloves with a denim dress; a fancy hat with jeans and a flannel shirt; balled-up polyester pants suits; and so forth.
- Greet the guests at the door wearing a ratty nightgown or pajamas; an old, faded robe; mismatched socks; hair in curlers; and so forth.

Decorations

- Scour garage sales and flea markets for *really* tacky decorations, such as pink plastic flamingos or plastic pinwheels that can be placed along your front walkway to greet your guests as they arrive.
- A garage is a wonderfully suited venue for a tacky party! Decorate it in the gaudiest, tackiest way possible: toilet paper "streamers"; a tattered blanket for a tablecloth; paper towels as napkins; metal and plastic tableware mixed; an assortment of odd glasses, some with lipstick marks on the rims and dirty fingerprints; empty soup cans as "cups"; broken Christmas ornaments hung on silk or fresh plants; cups and glasses with company logos; black velvet toreador pictures on the walls; and so on.
- Make a "tacky" centerpiece for the table: a "drippy" paint can filled with weeds or dead flowers or a perfectly awful vase with dusty, plastic flowers.

Fun Stuff

- Everyone should act as "tacky" as possible: their manners; eating habits; scratching themselves in obnoxious places; picking their noses; and so forth (this is a teen party, remember!).
- In addition to normal birthday gifts, have a "tacky gift exchange" with tacky, tasteless gifts, such as an enema kit. (Gifts should be wrapped in old wrinkled holiday paper, newspaper, or bags with logos.)
- Give prizes for the tackiest outfits and the tackiest behavior.
- Videotape the party from start to finish, then show the tape at the end of the party while everyone is enjoying dessert.

 **A tip.** This is a great party theme for a teen's birthday; the guests will surprise you with their clever "tacky wear."

Party Fare

- If you're serving a light lunch, serve "tacky food" in "tacky containers," such as bologna slices and hard bread, along with "real" food served on decent paper plates (see Chapter 44 for real food ideas.)
- Serve generic brands of beverages.
- Serve birthday cake with smeared icing and misspelled words written with tacky printing or writing. Serve with "non-tacky" ice cream.

21st
Birthday Party

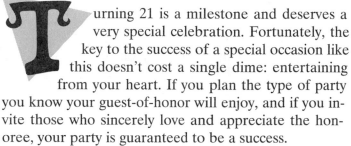

Turning 21 is a milestone and deserves a very special celebration. Fortunately, the key to the success of a special occasion like this doesn't cost a single dime: entertaining from your heart. If you plan the type of party you know your guest-of-honor will enjoy, and if you invite those who sincerely love and appreciate the honoree, your party is guaranteed to be a success.

The trick is to plan one of these celebrations on a small budget, and there are several party themes that will fill this bill. You can plan a "Roast" (see Chapter 4) where friends and family members good-naturedly roast the honored guest, or you can plan a very special evening with a "This Is Your Life" theme (also in Chapter 4). As you will see when you check out the requirements for these two themes, very little expense is involved in either of them.

Other at-home party themes include:

- Hawaiian Luau (see Chapter 36)
- Cruise Ship Formal Night Dinner Party (see Chapter 40)
- A Tailgate Party (see Chapter 37)
- An Informal Dinner Party (see Chapter 39)

Invitations

Create fake IDs on your computer that include the guest-of-honor's photo and the fact that he or she is 21 years old as of the day of the party. Print the party invitations on the reverse side of these IDs.

Decorations

Party supply stores sell decorations specifically designed for a 21st birthday party, of course; otherwise, inexpensive balloons and colorful crepe paper streamers will provide a festive venue, whatever your theme.

Fun Stuff

- Unless you're planning a "This Is Your Life" party, gather up photos, slides, and videos of the guest-of-honor as he or she was growing up; have them transferred onto a videotape, along with "toasts" from friends and relatives, including everyone present at the party, plus a few childhood classmates, junior high and high school teachers, his Pop Warner football coach, and so forth.
- Ask the guests to come dressed as their parents at age 21. Give prizes for "Most Authentic," "Silliest," and "Most Dramatic."

Party Fare

- A "Roast" or "This Is Your Life" party can get by with a birthday cake or an ice cream sundae bar. The other suggested themes include their own unique food and drink, as described in each of the referenced chapters.
- A toast is a must, whether you serve champagne or sparkling cider; however, it has been suggested that only nonalcoholic beverages be served, because many of the guests will undoubtedly still be under age.

Adult Birthday Parties

A n adult birthday party can be anything from a dessert and coffee get-together, to a casual dinner, to a formal sit-down dinner. You can incorporate many of the party themes in this book, from Hawaiian Luau (Chapter 36) to a Cruise Ship Formal Night Dinner Party (Chapter 40).

Invitations

See the specific theme chapters for suggestions or Chapter 1 for all-purpose ideas, depending on the formality of the party.

Decorations

Balloons and crepe paper streamers are festive, yet affordable, ways to decorate your party site, along with an eye-catching decorated cake, of course, which is usually placed in the center of the serving table.

Fun Stuff

- See Chapter 4 for games and activities, depending on the party's theme. For an 80th birthday, for example, a "This Is Your Life" surprise may be appropriate, or for your brother's 30th, you may want to plan a "Birthday Roast."
- Of course, the opening of gifts is the highlight of any birthday party.

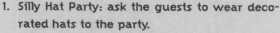

Optional themes for
an affordable adult birthday party:

1. Silly Hat Party: ask the guests to wear decorated hats to the party.
2. Costume Party: ask the guests to wear costumes based on a certain movie, such as *Star
Trek*, or a certain decade, such as the 60's, or
you can host a "masked ball" where the guests
arrive in "formal attire" and decorated masks.
3. Other novelty themes included in this book,
such as a Winter Beach Party (Chapter 15), a
Tailgate Party (Chapter 37) or a Video Scavenger Hunt (Chapter 38).

Party Fare

- Casual and formal menus are included in Chapter 44. Drink recipes are found in Chapter 42.
- A birthday cake is usually an essential element to any adult party, and for anyone turning age 75 on, it's important to place the correct number of candles on the cake. It's a lot of fun to turn the lights off and enter the room with a "flaming cake"; the trick is to get all the candles lit before some of them start to burn down. One solution is to have several candle lighters available, so each can light 15 or 20 candles. Another solution is to use tall, slender candles that don't burn down as fast.

Small-Budget Holiday Parties

When the holidays roll around, we're inspired to host awesome parties, but not if they'll break the bank. What we need are affordable ideas that are just as much fun as the expensive kind! And that's exactly what you'll find in this section: affordable holiday party ideas.

Combine the ideas with a few of the creative small-budget recipes in this book and you'll have a winner. Enjoy!

New Year's Eve Party

New Year's Eve is a nostalgic, emotionally charged night of the year when close friends get together to celebrate the anticipation of a better year ahead. The problem with hosting a New Year's Eve party, however, is that it can be a costly affair, by the time you buy all the liquor and provide exciting appetizers and desserts. There is a brilliant solution to this problem, however: Make it a "Wine and Cheese Tasting Party," where it's perfectly proper etiquette to ask each guest (or couple) to bring a bottle of their favorite wine and a complementary cheese for tasting. That way, all you'll need to provide are an array of crackers and a fancy, affordable dessert.

Invitations

- Enlarge and copy the month of December from your calendar. Fill in "December 31" with the place and time of the party. Make copies and roll the sheet into a scroll, tie with a ribbon and hand-deliver or mail.
- Create "New Year's Resolutions" sheets, with the party invitation printed across the top. This can be computer-generated or designed by hand and duplicated on a copy machine. Roll the sheets into a scroll, tie with ribbons, and hand-deliver. Ask the guests to fill out the sheets and bring them to the party.

Costumes

- The dress may range in formality from "dressy casual" to a "black-and-white" party where the guests dress up in black tuxedos and black or white evening gowns.
- New Year's Eve masquerade parties are also trendy in certain communities around the country.

Decorations

- Remove ornaments and all Christmasy decorations from your Christmas tree and transform it into a "New Year's Tree" by adding glass icicles, bright party streamers, noise-makers, and a decorated party hat for the top of the tree.
- Decorate the site with balloons and streamers, and don't forget the hats, horns, and plenty of confetti!
- Turn the lights down low, light the candles, and add strings of tiny white Christmas lights to lend a magical quality to the evening.
- For an eye-catching table centerpiece, set a silver bucket filled with ice and full wine bottles (so generously donated by your guests), arranged at angles to look like flowers blooming in a pot.

Fun Stuff

- While you're waiting for that ever-elusive stroke of midnight, fill the time by hosting a wine tasting contest, even if tongue-in-cheek. Ask your guests to serve as wine judges as they rank each wine according to:

    1. Color (Clear? Pale? Rich?)
    2. Bouquet (Fruity? Delicate? Pungent?)
    3. Taste (Dry? Smooth? Full-bodied?)

- If you should be so fortunate as to have a legitimate wine connoisseur among your guests, take advantage of the person's expertise by having him or her introduce the wines as they are served, explaining their origins and qualities.
- Ask the guests to count their blessings from the year past and reveal their New Year's resolutions.

- Make a "joyful noise" at midnight—anything goes (except guns!): horns; car horns; fireworks (where legal); and sing "Auld Lang Syne" (provide a few kazoos for those who can't remember the words!) Provide each guest with one party horn and one paper blowout (the party toy that looks like a party horn, but shoots out a colorful paper tube when blown).
- Before the party, blow up balloons and fill them with confetti. At the stroke of midnight, burst them and let the confetti fly!

Party Fare

- During the wine tasting contest, most of the bottles will have been opened and can be served with the various cheeses provided by your guests, along with the crackers you have provided.
- If you would like and can afford it, you can also provide fresh strawberries and seedless grapes.
- As the midnight hour approaches, turn off all the lights, blast a little march music and enter the room carrying Baked Alaska (see Chapter 44), complete with lighted sparklers or long, tapered white candles. Baked Alaska, although a relatively inexpensive dessert to make, has always been considered a glamorous dessert, even before the cruise ships began to feature their Baked Alaska Nights.

A tip.

- It's a good idea to begin your New Year's Eve party at 8 or 9p.m. Otherwise, the evening drags on too long.
- Be sure to serve each wine at its required temperature. For example, a Burgundy wine should be served at room temperature, while a white wine should be chilled but not icy. Red wines should be opened an hour or more before serving, allowing them to breathe.
- Host beware: If a guest has had a little too much alcohol, it's up to you to see that he arrives home safe and sound. Ask someone to drive him home; call a cab; or drive him home yourself. He can always retrieve his car the next day.

Valentine's Day

Valentine's Day is a lovely excuse to host a party, which doesn't need to be expensive to be a very special, romantic affair.

Invitations

Purchase an inexpensive box of children's Valentines to use as party invitations. Print the invitation on the back of each Valentine; mail or hand-deliver.

Costumes

Encourage everyone to wear red or pink.

Decorations

- Decorate with large red, white, and pink hearts cut from construction paper, embellished with red ribbons and white paper lace.
- Invert a colander and fill with red heart-shaped lollipops inserted into the holes. Tie each lollipop at its neck with a red ribbon.
- Set small red heart-shaped boxes of chocolates in the center of each place setting as party favors.
- Place clusters of non-helium red balloons around the room; on the serving table; or tied in groups of three to the backs of chairs.

- Add red, white, and pink crepe paper streamers and a couple balloons to the lamppost in the front yard, the entryway, and doorways.
- Turn off *all* the lights and give the room a romantic glow with strings of tiny white Christmas tree lights and as many red, pink, and white candles as you can afford.

Fun Stuff

- Ask several couples to tell how they met and fell in love; ask any newly engaged or newly married couples the same questions, along with the juicy details of the marriage proposal! (Who proposed? Where were they when it happened? What was the immediate response? How long before they were married?)
- Divide into two teams. See how many songs each team can *sing* correctly that have the word heart in them.
- See how many legitimate words the guests can make out of the words Valentine's Day in five minutes. (Use a timer.)
- Have the guests guess how many candy hearts are in a clear glass container. The winner is presented with the container of candy hearts as a prize.
- Play the Newlywed/Oldywed Game (see Chapter 4).
- Convert your patio or any tile or vinyl floored room into a romantic "nightclub" by clearing away the furniture to provide after-dinner dancing. String small white lights and a few balloons and all you'll need is some "slow-dancin'" romantic music, such as Roberta Flack's "The First Time Ever I Saw Your Face" or Tony Bennett's "My Funny Valentine."

Party Fare

- You may serve an elegant, romantic, candlelight sit-down dinner (see Chapter 44), or an informal supper buffet with as many affordable red foods as possible, such as *red* gelatin salads; spaghetti with *red* tomato sauce; fresh *red* strawberries, *red* fruit punch, and so forth.
- Serve decorated heart-shaped cookies or a heart-shaped cake.

Mother's Day Luncheon

Mother's Day is one of those holidays where the best gifts don't cost a thing: hugs and verbal expressions of our love. As obvious as this may seem, mothers don't always receive these endearments throughout the year, especially from their adult children. So, it isn't how much you spend on your Mom, but how much love and appreciation you're able to express to her on her special day.

Decorations

Decorate the table with flowers or create a display of framed photos of Mom and her kids as you were growing up. Add candles, a little lace and ribbon, and you'll have a lovely nostalgic centerpiece.

Fun Stuff

- Present Mom with gifts, cut flowers or a corsage, and mushy cards.
- Show a "Nostalgia Video Show" composed of old photos, home movies, and videotapes that have been transferred to a single videotape. Gather up all the heart-tugging photos you can find of Mom with you when you were a baby, or Mom with her arms around your brother when his team won the regional basketball finals, or Mom holding her new granddaughter in the hospital right after she was born. Moms are sentimental creatures, so you're guaranteed to bring a tear to her eye as she views

this tape. Of course, the tape will be given to her as a gift to enjoy over and over again.

- Award your Mom a "Certificate of Honor" or an award of "Special Achievement." These can be hand-printed on parchment paper or created on your computer.
- Another poignant activity is to have each child read a poem he or she has composed in advance, or tell about the one favorite memory of her as the child was growing up.

 **A tip.** Daddies: If your children are young and you're trying to plan a party for Mommy on their behalf, what she'll appreciate most are a few cards or gifts the children have made themselves.

Party Fare

- If you provide Mom with a home-cooked luncheon, cut down on the costs by sharing the cooking duties with your siblings. One child can bring a salad, another a tray of finger sandwiches, and another one of Mom's favorite desserts.
- Or, if you decide to take Mom out to lunch, you can split the bill, of course.

Father's Day Barbecue Bash

ere's another one of those sentimental holidays where the best gifts are free: expression of your love and appreciation. Like mothers, fathers may not receive hugs and verbal expressions of love throughout the year, especially from their grown children who may live in other cities or states.

Fun Stuff

- Present Dad with thoughtful gifts and cards, along with a few humorous gifts as well, such as the ugliest or silliest tie you can find (try your local thrift shop). Note: Have each child decorate a solid-colored baseball cap as a gift for Dad; designs, such as a fishing pole or golf club, can be drawn with felt-tip pens or Dad's nickname can be printed or written across the bill.
- Dad will appreciate a "Nostalgia Video Show" as much as Mom does on Mother's Day. (See Chapter 21)
- Have each child relate his favorite memory of Dad as the child was growing up. I heard of one case where each of the children made a list of "20 Things I Learned from My Father." These lists were read out loud, including one from a grown child who wasn't able to attend. Note: Place these lists in a notebook and give them to Dad as a special gift.

Party Fare

- Barbecue chicken, hamburgers, and hot dogs, served with affordable side dishes, such as homemade potato salad, tossed salad, and Dad's favorite dessert.

- Whatever you decide to do for Dad, he'll appreciate it, just so he has your undivided attention for one day a year. The fact that you've given up your Sunday to spend it with him is what really counts.
- Mommies: If your children are young, have them make homemade gifts or cards for Dad; they will mean more than anything store bought.

Summer Holiday Picnics (Memorial Day, 4th of July, Labor Day)

A good old-fashioned picnic is in order for any of these holidays. It can be an affordable get-together, especially if the guests bring food. Include a list of suggested food dishes in the invitations. If you provide the meat, such as fried chicken, hamburgers, or hot dogs, let the guests bring the salads, potato chips, baked beans, watermelon, desserts, and so forth.

Invitations

- Send a hand-crafted novelty invitation, such as a miniature basket, lined with a tiny piece of red checkered fabric, with the invitation tucked inside.
- Hand-print or computer-generate the invitation. Attach a tiny American flag to the invitation, tying it to one corner with a narrow red ribbon. Hand-deliver to save on postage.
- For a Labor Day Picnic, attach the invitation to the Help Wanted page from your newspaper and hand-deliver.
- Optional: Ask your guests to wear decorated hats to the picnic.

Decorations

- Use a red, white, and blue theme: American flags, of course, plus crepe paper streamers and balloons.
- Cover the picnic tables with red-and-white checkered tablecloths or old quilts.

- Tie non-helium balloon "bouquets" to the ends of the picnic tables.
- Table centerpiece ideas:
  1. Insert small American flags into a watermelon that has been cut in half lengthwise.
  2. Place 4-inch pots of blooming red geraniums inside white paper lunch sacks; roll down the top of each sack, creating a "collar"; tie a "necktie" around the "collar" with a 2-inch wide blue ribbon.
  3. For Labor Day, create a table centerpiece from workers' tools (plumber's helper, wrenches, hammers, saws, paint brushes, and so forth.)

Fun Stuff

- Play old-fashioned summer picnic games:

  Nail-Pounding Contest, Horseshoe Competition, Egg Toss or Water Balloon Toss, Sack Race, Three-Legged Race, Wheelbarrow Race, Kick-the-Shoe Contest, Flag Football, Frisbee Contest, Softball, Tug-of-War, and Volleyball.
- The 4th of July calls for a few fireworks after dark, if they are legal in your city.
- If you've asked your guests to wear decorated hats, have a fashion parade to show off their hats while you play recorded John Philip Sousa march music. Give prizes for the "Most Patriotic," "Most Creative," and so forth.

Party Fare

- Serve traditional picnic fare: barbecued chicken, hamburgers or hot dogs, potato salad, red gelatin salad, fresh strawberries, coleslaw, baked beans, corn on the cob, watermelon, seedless grapes, potato chips, chocolate cake or cupcakes, homemade ice cream, and plenty of ice-cold beer and soda.
- Instead of paper plates, provide decorated "lunch buckets" (inexpensive white cardboard paint buckets, available from your discount hardware store, tied with red, white, and blue ribbons, or red cord for "handles").

Don't forget all the "gear":

- Bottle opener.
- Plastic plates (or the decorated buckets), cups, tablecloth, tableware.
- Condiments: salt, pepper, catsup, mustard, pickle relish, olives, pickles, seasonings.
- Plenty of ice.
- Paper towels and paper napkins.
- Matches.
- Barbecue grill and tools.
- Serving spoons and forks.
- Pot holders or barbecue mitts.
- Plenty of trash bags.
- Sharp cutting knives.
- Aluminum foil.
- Blankets.
- Folding lawn chairs and/or "stadium seats" with backrests (to attach to the picnic bench seats).
- Insect repellant.
- Citronella candles, to ward off the mosquitoes in the first place!
- Suntan lotion.
- Sports equipment.

- For the 4th of July, decorate the desserts with American flags and sparklers; light the sparklers just before serving.

Halloween Parties

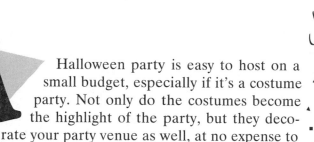

A Halloween party is easy to host on a small budget, especially if it's a costume party. Not only do the costumes become the highlight of the party, but they decorate your party venue as well, at no expense to you whatsoever!

If you're hosting an adult costume party, you may want to use a Masquerade Party theme that requires the guests to wear masks in addition to their costumes. This adds interest to the party as the guests try to guess who's who.

Invitations

- For a children's party, cut black poster board into the shape of a bat; write the invitation on back of the "bat" and mail. Be sure to ask the children to arrive in costume.
- For an adult party, send or hand-deliver to each guest an inexpensive black mask with an invitation attached. Ask your guests to wear costumes and the masks to the party.

Costumes

- Everyone is in costume.
- Greet your guests at the door wearing an inexpensive mummy costume; wrap yourself up from head to toe with gauze bandages or strips of old white sheets. Leave holes for your mouth, nose and eyes.

Decorations

- Decorate the yard with large orange plastic "trash sack pumpkins" (readily available and quite affordable) filled with scrunched-up newspapers; and white plastic trash sack "ghosts" suspended from the trees and front doorway. Line the walkway with "ghostly" luminaries (see Chapter 2).
- String tiny white Christmas lights across your front porch or from tree to tree in a spider web design. Add big black spiders, available at party supply stores, or make your own from black construction paper.
- Arrange cattails, milkweed, and dried pods, along with any weeds you can find, in a wicker basket. Add gourds, small pumpkins, and squashes around the base of the basket.
- Suspend an ordinary broom from the ceiling; place a stuffed animal on the broom, so he is riding it. Let your animal wear a Halloween mask, or a costume if you can find one for him.
- Give your room a spooky glow by replacing your standard white light bulbs with green bulbs.
- Suspend black bats and spiders (cut from construction paper) from the ceiling.
- Cover the top of your serving table with a "ghost" (a white sheet with a head, arms and a puffy body filled with crushed tissue paper.) Place the food dishes *on* the ghost: one on the face, one on each of the ghost's hands, and the main dish in the center of the ghost's stomach.

Fun Stuff

- A costume party needs prizes for the "Most Creative," "Scariest," "Cutest," and so forth. For the children, have a "Costume Parade" where they parade around the house, yard, or neighborhood, showing off their costumes. For the adults, take them on a hay ride around town.
- Bobbing for Doughnuts or Apples: Hang sturdy doughnuts (glazed or buttermilk work best) from the ceiling with strings. Have the guests hold their hands behind their backs as they bob for the doughnuts, trying to tear one loose

from its string. Or, fill a large galvanized wash tub full of small Red Delicious apples and, using only their mouths, give the guests each one chance to grab an apple in their teeth (no hands allowed.)

- "Apple Biting Contest": suspend apples from the ceiling by strings. Divide the guests up into pairs, two children per apple. Ask the children to place their hands behind their backs and at a given signal begin to bite their apples. The object is to bite the apple down to its core. The difficulty, of course, is to keep the apple from swinging around as they try to take bites. The pair who has chewed their apple closest to the core at the end of three minutes is declared the winner.

- "Old Dead Joe's Cave: This is a deliciously scary activity for the *older* kids. The object is to set up a darkened room ahead of time where Old Dead Joe's "guts," "eyes," "tongue," and so forth, are placed in bowls. If the children are brave enough, they are blindfolded and allowed to enter the cave, one child at a time. You, as gracious host, must lead the child from bowl to scary bowl, telling him to dip his hands into the bowl to feel the contents. The rest of the children sit quietly and listen intently to the screams and squeals of the child being led through the cave. Here are old dead Joe's "body parts" that need to be assembled ahead of time:

  - Old Dead Joe's Guts – A large bowl filled with wet, slimy noodles.
  - Old Dead Joe's Heart – A large peeled tomato.
  - Old Dead Joe's Eyes – A small, shallow bowl of water containing two large grapes.
  - Old Dead Joe's Teeth – A metal pot or bowl filled with small rocks or candy corn.
  - Old Dead Joe's Hair – A human hair wig sitting on a wig stand.
  - Old Dead Joe's Tongue – A slimy, wet piece of raw beef liver sitting in a shallow bowl of warm water.
  - Old Dead Joe's Bones – Old steak bones or any kind of bones.
  - Old Dead Joe's Ears – Two halves of an artichoke (with the sharp tips cut off).

- Old Dead Joe's Nose – A raw potato carved into the shape of a nose.
- Old Dead Joe's Fingers – Cold hot dogs.
- Old Dead Joe's Blood – A crock pot full of warm tomato juice.

Have a towel ready to wrap around the child's hands after he has dipped them in the "blood." As you exit the cave with the child, make a big deal out of saying, "Hurry, Jimmy, let's wash the blood off in the sink – don't let the blood drip on the floor."

Use a small flashlight to guide your way through the dark room. Of course, the child will be blindfolded, but you'll need a little bit of light to be able to dip his hands in and out of the bowls.

- Have your co-host videotape all the festivities (including the visits to Old Dead Joe's Cave) and show it near the end of the party.

Party Fare

For a children's party:

- Place a "ghost" at each place setting as a party favor (wrap a large round lollipop with a circle cut from a white plastic garbage bag, tie at the "neck" with a black ribbon, and draw large "ghostly" eyes, using black felt tip marker.)
- Old Dead Joe's eyeballs
  - 10 hard-boiled eggs
  - 6 ounces whipped cream cheese
  - One green olive per eyeball
  - Toothpick and red food coloring

  Slice the eggs in half; discard the yolks. Fill with cream cheese, until the cheese "bulges" above the rim of the egg. Place a green olive on top of the cream cheese, with the red "eye" facing up. Use the toothpick to dribble red food coloring down the sides of the cream cheese, to look like a bloodshot eye.

- Old Dead Joe's toes
  - 2 packages ready-made sugar cookie dough mix
  - 1 can cashew nuts
  - Green food coloring

Roll the dough into toe-shaped pieces. Press one cashew nut into the end of each "toe" to form a "toenail." Bake as directed. When baked, use green food coloring to color the "toenails."

- Old Dead Joe's teeth: candy corn.
- Old Dead Joe's Favorite Cupcake Spiders (see Chapter 43) or Old Dead Joe's Favorite Worm Cake — bake a chocolate sheet cake; top it with crumbled Oreo cookies; add gummy worms "crawling" out of the cake.

For an adult party

- Hollow out small pumpkins to use as serving bowls.
- Snack Mix*
- Chip n' Dip: Add green food coloring to Horseradish Crab Dip*
- Halloween Potato Salad (see Tomato Flower Potato Salad*)
- Halloween Hamburger Pie (see Hamburger Pie*)
- Pumpkin pizzas (see "Personalized Pizzas," Chapter 43): Make pumpkin faces with:
  - Eyes: Button mushrooms, black olives, or cucumber slices.
  - Nose: Jalapeno pepper or carrot piece.
  - Lips: Red pepper ring or apple peel.
- Serve Caramel Apples for dessert:
  - 1 small McIntosh apple per guest
  - 2 pounds store-bought caramels per ten apples
  - 4 tablespoons water
  - 1 cup chopped peanuts
  - 1 wooden skewer per apple

Place apples in metal cupcake liners. Remove the apple stems and insert skewers. Melt caramels with the water in microwave until smooth and creamy. Dip the apples in the caramel mixture, then roll in chopped peanuts, return to the cupcake liners and refrigerate until ready to serve.

*Indicates recipe given in Chapter 44.

For a children's or adult party:

- "Witches Brew": Combine pineapple juice, scoops of orange sherbet, and cold ginger ale. (This punch will "bubble and foam" when you pour the carbonated soda over the sherbet.) Instead of adding ice, float a frozen "hand." (Fill a plastic glove with water, close the "wrist" with a tight rubber band, and freeze. When ready to use, dip briefly in warm water to loosen the glove, slide the hand out of the glove and add it to the "Witches Brew.")

Christmas Parties

A Christmas party can be easy and inexpensive to host if you take advantage of your existing Christmas decorations and you don't get carried away with the food and drink.

Invitations

Computer-generate your invitations and send via e-mail or fax, or tie them to the necks of Christmas candy canes and hand-deliver.

Decorations

- Line your walkway with luminaries (see Chapter 2).
- Decorate your home with traditional Christmas symbols, such as evergreen garlands, red and white candles, pine cone wreaths, and a lighted Christmas tree.
- Hang plenty of mistletoe, suspended from ceilings and doorways.
- Cover your serving tables with bright red or green felt or overlay several Christmas tablecloths.
- Create a table centerpiece by filling a wicker basket with pyracantha berries and six or eight white candles of various heights, or arrange gift-wrapped boxes around sprays of evergreen boughs dotted with tiny white Christmas tree lights.
- Wrap Christmas napkins around the silverware and tie with gold metallic ribbon.

Fun Stuff

- If your celebration is a family party that takes place on Christmas Eve, it's traditional to light the candles on the Advent Wreath, a circle of greenery around which four red candles are equally spaced.
- Another family tradition is to attend a Christmas Eve or Christmas morning church service together, followed by opening of gifts. (Of course, the small children believe their gifts are from Santa.)
- Caravan together to see holiday lights or go caroling around the neighborhood, returning for dessert and one of the beverages mentioned in Party Fare (page 103).
- Ask your guests to bring wrapped gifts with no gift tags (have a spending limit, such as $5). Have the guests open the gifts, one at a time. After a gift has been opened, give the guest the option of keeping the gift, selecting another from the pile, or "robbing" another guest of his gift. Each guest has three "steals" until the last gift has been opened.

 **A tip.**

- Fill the house with fragrance by simmering cinnamon sticks in a potpourri pot.
- Pick up a turkey for free during November. Look for grocery stores offering a free turkey if you spend a certain amount at their store; freeze the turkey for your Christmas party.
- You can host a Christmas party *after* Christmas, during the lull between Christmas Day and New Year's when people aren't quite as busy.

Party Fare

- There are three ways to keep the costs down:
  1. Serve a buffet-style meal. Provide only the meat and beverages; let your guests fill in the side dishes "potluck style."
  2. Serve lighter fare, such as snacks and appetizers only, a lighter buffet, or dessert only.

3. Go together with several friends or family members to host a progressive dinner, which takes place in several homes with a different course being served in each home. A Christmas progressive dinner is a very affordable option, with dessert and holiday coffees served at the last house. A progressive dinner not only distributes the cost of the party, but it gives the guests a chance to enjoy the Christmas decorations in each home.

• Beverages: Hot cider, specialty coffees, hot chocolate, "Comforting Christmas Nog," or "Wonderful Wassail" (see Chapter 42).

Part

Small-Budget
Special Occasion Parties

Special life events, such as an engagement, a retirement, or a wedding anniversary, call for special celebrations. Nurturing relationships with friends and family is another reason why you may want to host a special party from time to time, such as a luau, a wine tasting party, or a formal dinner party.

Wouldn't it be nice if we could host these special parties without spending a lot of money? There are ways, my friends, and this section is filled with creative ideas for hosting these parties on a small budget.

Post-Prom Party

Host a party for the kids after the prom; keep it as formal as possible without breaking the bank. They will appreciate being able to prolong the evening's fun by having someplace to go where they can reminisce, enjoy special eats, and each other's company.

Invitations

Create calligraphied invitations, printed on white parchment paper; computer-generate using a fancy, italicized font; or simply extend the invitations in person or over the telephone.

Decorations

- This will be an after-dark party, so line your driveway or entryway with homemade luminaries (see Chapter 2).
- Set an elegant table with your best linen, silver, china, and crystal, including long-stemmed glasses for toasting. Add long-stemmed candles and table art (see Chapter 2) that complements the prom's theme or includes the school's colors.
- Decorate the rest of the party site with balloons tied with crinkle-tie ribbon, suspended from the chandelier, set in shallow bowls around the room, and attached to doorways and stairways.
- If you have cut flowers or flowering shrubs available for free from your garden, set a few arrangements around the room.

- Finally, the best way to soften the room and give it an elegant, romantic ambience is to turn the lights down low and add tiny white Christmas tree lights throughout. Hang them over doorways and windows, wrap them around silk trees or plants, or trail them down the center of your serving table.
- Make place cards by cutting 3 1/2-inch squares of heavy paper, using a mat knife. Lightly score the cards in the center, then fold them along the scored crease. Write the guests' names with a fine felt-tip pen.

 **Don't serve alcoholic beverages.**

Fun Stuff

- Take an instant photo of each couple; send the photo home in a frame you have constructed beforehand from poster board.
- Toast any graduates present with sparkling cider.

Party Fare

- Depending on how late you plan the party, serve a "Midnight Buffet" or a "Dessert Buffet" (see Chapters 44 and 41 for menu ideas.) Stay away from any foods that are drippy or messy.

Graduation Party

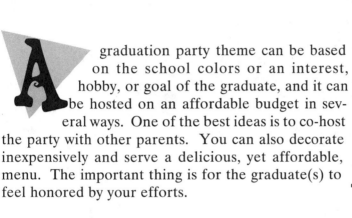

A graduation party theme can be based on the school colors or an interest, hobby, or goal of the graduate, and it can be hosted on an affordable budget in several ways. One of the best ideas is to co-host the party with other parents. You can also decorate inexpensively and serve a delicious, yet affordable, menu. The important thing is for the graduate(s) to feel honored by your efforts.

Invitations

- Hand-deliver rolled-up parchment scrolls (diplomas) tied with narrow ribbon with the invitation printed inside.
- Make color copies of a photo of the school mascot or the honored guest as an elementary student. Write the invitation on the back.

Decorations

- Decorate with over sized rolled-up diplomas and mortarboards, complete with dangling tassels.
- Decorate the serving table with memorabilia: prom photos, textbooks, pom-poms, pennants, copies of yearbooks, and so forth.
- Enlarge the graduate's yearbook photo to display on an easel.
- Splash the school colors around the room with crepe paper and non-helium balloons.

Fun Stuff

- Ask the school mascot to make a surprise appearance.
- Watch videotapes of the school's senior prom, sports events, and the graduation ceremony itself.
- Go around the room and complete this sentence relating to the graduate: "Most Likely to _____."

- It's important to involve your graduate in the party plans.
- Don't serve alcohol at a high school graduation party.

Party Fare

- Serve the graduate's favorite food, which will probably be make-your-own tacos, pizza, spaghetti, giant deli sandwiches or barbecued hamburgers with all the trimmings.
- A decorated cake is a must, with the name(s) of the graduates written in icing.
- Toasts are in order; let the guests toast with sparkling cider or party punch.

Engagement Celebrations

The purpose of an engagement party, of course, is to celebrate the couple's engagement, but it's also a chance for the two families to meet and get to know each other. It can be a formal or informal get-together and hosted and attended by either friends or family. Traditionally, however, it is a formal party hosted by the bride's or groom's parents and attended by members of the couple's families.

Fortunately, an engagement party is such an exciting romantic affair that it's guaranteed to be a success in spite of your small budget. Here are a few affordable engagement celebration themes to consider:

Formal Party Themes

Elegant Sit-Down Engagement Dinner

This party is limited to members of the bride's and groom's families. See Chapter 44 for a formal, yet affordable, dinner menu.

Candlelight and Roses Dessert Party

This is an excellent choice if you would like to host a formal party, but you don't have the funds to plan a sit-down dinner. The ambience is created with candles, fresh or silk roses, swirling tulle netting, and delicate ribbons. String tiny all-white Christmas lights along the tables, around plants or garlands and over doorways. This theme works best, of course, as an evening affair.

Serve a congratulatory cake, plus one or more of your personal, yet affordable, dessert favorites. Or, see Chapter 44 for affordable dessert ideas, including Baked Alaska.

Informal Party Themes

Country-Western Barbecue

Drag out your cowboy boots, 10-gallon hats, and bandannas for this party, and encourage your guests to get into the spirit by wearing their western outfits, too.

Decorate with lariats, cowboy hats, saddles, branding irons, wagon wheels, singletrees, potted cactus plants, hay bales, and red-checkered tablecloths.

Provide taped music for a little country-western dancing after you eat. By the time your guests have done a couple line-dances and tried the Macarena, they'll be into the spirit of the party and providing their own entertainment.

See the Barbecue Bash menu described in Chapter 22.

Note: Ask each guest to bring a side dish; that way you'll only need to furnish meat for the barbecue.

Remember When? Party

Collect memorabilia from the couple's past to use as decorations: baby pictures, Little League uniforms, cheer-leading pom-poms, old high school or college yearbooks, scrapbooks, pennants, awards, trophies, and so forth. Dress up two teddy bears (preferably the bride's and groom's own childhood bears, if they still exist). Create a veil for the "bride bear" out of white tulle netting and a top hat for the "groom bear" from black construction paper. It doesn't matter if the top hat and veil aren't perfect; it's the thought that counts!

If the party is attended by family members who have never met, a "Photo Corner" can be set up with wedding photographs of the bride's and groom's parents, grandparents, aunts, uncles, brothers, and sisters. This nostalgic corner will be a focal point throughout the party as relatives from both sides gather around to compare wedding fashions and talk about their own engagements and wedding ceremonies.

You may even be able to add a display of wedding memorabilia, such as the grandmothers' wedding gowns, fans, shoes, hair combs, or bridal veils. If possible, "model" the gowns on a dressmaker's form or a store mannequin.

A Remember When? Slide or Video Show (see later in this chapter) will be appreciated by all.

You can serve any of the informal menus in Chapter 44 or coffee and cake only.

Invitations

- For a formal party, make a master invitation, using black ink and a calligraphy pen. Copy the master onto parchment paper at a copy shop. Roll each piece of parchment into a scroll, tie with a narrow ribbon, and hand-deliver.
- For an informal party, make copies of the couple's engagement photo on a color copy machine, using heavyweight paper. Then run these sheets through a copier, printing the party invitation on the back of each photo. Cut each into about 15 irregular pieces to form a jigsaw puzzle. Enclose the pieces in an envelope addressed to each guest. Of course, the guest will have to put the puzzle together in order to figure it out.

Fun Stuff

Remember When? Slide or Video Show

Round up photos, slides, videos, and home movies of the bride and groom, from their babyhood to present day, and have them converted to slides or a single videotape. Arrange them in chronological order: the bride as a baby, the groom as a baby, the bride as a toddler, the groom as a toddler, the bride as a 10-year-old, the groom as a 10-year old, the bride as a junior high student, the groom as a junior high student, and so forth, through their high school and college days, ending finally with their engagement photo.

We composed one of these "Remember When?" slide shows for our daughter and son-in-law's party, using a "dissolve" feature whereby one picture gradually disappears as the next one appears, creating a continuous story. The room was darkened during this slide presentation while a friend of ours sang "Sunrise, Sunset" as she accompanied herself on the guitar.

Dress the Bride and Groom

The men take the groom into one room and the women take the bride into another. Everyone is furnished with plenty of crepe paper;

tissue paper; black, white, and colored poster paper; fabric scraps; pieces of lace and braid and buttons; plus felt tip markers, staplers, tape, and safety pins. The men and women are given 20 minutes to "dress" the couple, fashioning a gown and veil for the bride and a suit or tuxedo for the groom.

Once the bride and groom are dressed and ready to "get married," they walk arm-in-arm "down the aisle" to the strains of everyone singing or humming "Here Comes the Bride." This is a photo opp you won't want to miss, so be sure to have plenty of film on hand.

- The Newlywed Game, described in Chapter 4, is a popular game for one of these parties.
- See my books, *Complete Book of Wedding Showers* and *Big Book of Parties* for more engagement party ideas.
- For engagement toasts, see my book *Complete Book of Wedding Toasts*.

Party Fare

In addition to the menus included with the formal and informal themes described, you'll definitely need to provide a congratulatory cake with the couple's names written with icing.

Bachelor Parties

The trend in bachelor parties today is toward sports-oriented get-togethers, casino weekends, poker parties, and good old-fashioned roasts. The groom, best man, or groom's father may host the party, or it may be organized by all the guys who decide what they think would be the most fun.

Who should be invited to a bachelor party? All the adult male members of the wedding party, including the groomsmen and the ushers. I've also heard of several bachelor parties lately where the groom's sisters were also invited.

Here are some of the most popular and affordable ways to celebrate:

A "Roast"

- A roast usually follows a formal or informal dinner (see Chapter 44 for menu suggestions). The idea is to have a speaker's stand, called a "dais," located at one of the tables. The men take turns telling stories about the groom, "roasting" him by recounting the dumbest or most embarrassing things he's ever done. The key to the success of one of these parties is to be careful that you don't reveal anything *too* personal or humiliating. This is supposed to be a fun party, not a chance to pull skeletons out of the groom's closet!

- Be sure to end your roast on a sincere, poignant note, saying what a good friend he's been to you and so on, and, if you feel comfortable doing so, offering a toast to his bride.

- If you really want the roast to be a success, try to come up with a surprise guest: one of the groom's old high school buddies, a brother or college friend who flies in unexpectedly, or one of his teachers or professors who has some embarrassing story to tell about the groom.

Poker Party

- An informal night of poker, or any other card game, is a sure-fire choice for a successful bachelor party. Whether a rousing "Hearts" tournament or winner-take-all poker game, the men will enjoy the bonding and camaraderie.
- Furnish affordable snacks and appetizers (see Chapter 44), along with drinks and plenty of ice. The important thing is that everything can be eaten with the hands so the guys won't have to juggle plates and silverware during the competition.

 **A tip.**

- The one traditional element of a bachelor party is a toast by the groom to his bride as he stands, raises his glass and says, "To my bride!" Then the men stand and join him in the toast.
- Bachelor parties need very little, if anything, in the way of decorations.

Men's Night Out

- Make plans to attend a pay-for-your-own-ticket "macho movie," a boxing match, a live concert or a performance by your favorite comedian at a comedy club.
- You can also rent a movie or a live concert on videotape, or watch a pay-for-view boxing match in your own family room.

Sports Activity

An active sports-oriented get-together is one of the popular trends in bachelor parties. One reason is that they provide a way to blow off a little steam. After all, planning a wedding has become more hectic than ever and the physical activity is a good stress-reliever for all the guys, but especially for the groom. In fact, the more physical, the better the men seem to like it. For this idea to fit into your budget, however, the men must pay their own way. Here are choices to consider: tennis, golf, volleyball, horseshoes, bowling, pool or billiards, camping or backpacking, white water rafting, snow or water skiing, or fishing.

- Provide prizes or trophies for first, second, and third place or, in the case of a golf tournament, for example, you could give out prizes for "Closest to the Hole," "Longest Drive," and so on.
- It's important for you to eat together after the big event, whether it's just a hamburger in the clubhouse after golf or tennis, a stop at a restaurant on the way home, or a barbecue beside the water at the end of a day of fishing or rafting. Each man pays for his own meal.

Take Me Out to the Ball Game (a.k.a. "Tailgate Party")

A tailgate party is one in which each man buys his own ticket to the game. You provide the tailgate eats.

- Bring your gloves to a professional baseball game or, depending on the season, round up tickets to watch your favorite football, basketball, or hockey team play a home game. Of course, by "watching" instead of "participating," you won't get in as much physical activity, but it can still be a great time together.
- See Chapter 37 for Tailgate Party food ideas.

Bridal Showers

A bridal shower is usually attended by the bride's female family members and close friends, including her maid- or matron-of-honor and bridesmaids. The party is often hosted, in fact, by one of her attendants. The purpose of the party is to "shower" the bride with affection, support, and thoughtful, loving gifts.

Here are popular bridal showers that are fun, yet affordable:

Apron Shower

- The invitations can be written on the backs of miniature "aprons" cut from construction paper. Enclose blank recipe cards for the women to fill out and bring to the party, along with an apron; suggest a half-apron, floor-length party apron, barbecue apron, apron with humorous saying, or sewing or gardening smock.

- Place a freestanding coat rack, decorated with ribbons and balloons, next to the bride; hang a display of aprons, with cooking utensils and recipe cards protruding from their pockets.

- Build a "Lady's Maid," which is a decorated ironing board. One "arm" is a toilet plunger and the other a toilet bowl brush. A string mop is attached to the back of the board with the "hair" hanging over the top. Add a colander hat, scouring pad eyes, a small sponge nose, and a nail brush for the mouth. Tie an apron around her "waist" and tuck dish towels and potholders into the apron's pockets. Add a little costume jewelry and you'll definitely have a conversation piece.

119

Gourmet Cooking Shower

- Computer-generate the invitations by scanning a collage of pictures of cooking utensils. Be sure to add the names of the stores where the bride has registered.
- Decorate the room with anything cooking related, such as chefs' hats, a cookbook display, hanging garlic braids, or "bouquets" of kitchen utensils. Suspend an ordinary clothesline across the room to display anything that will attach easily to the line with clothespins.
- Use colorful dish towels as place mats and napkins.
- In addition to other games you may play, ask each guest to tell about her worst cooking disaster.

Linen Shower

- Sew miniature pillow cases; place the invitations inside the pillow cases and mail or hand-deliver. Include a list of the stores where the bride has registered for linens, along with the size of the couple's bed; colors of their bedroom, baths, and kitchen; and the size of their dining room table.
- Decorate the room by stringing a clothesline from one end to the other. As the bride opens her gifts, use clothespins to hang them on the clothesline, with cards attached.
- Decorate the cake with a miniature clothesline with tiny towels, pillow cases, and sheets attached with toy clothespins.

Special Times Shower

- Computer-generate the invitations. Scan a picture of a clock or watch on the front of the invitation. On the inside of the invitations assign a specific day, month, time of day, or season to each guest, requesting a suitable gift.
  For example:
  - "7 a.m."—coffee mug and a bag of gourmet coffee beans.
  - "Monday Morning"—a basket of detergents, spot removers, and so on for "laundry day."

- "July Afternoon"—swim fins, a beach towel, a Frisbee, and suntan lotion.
- "5 p.m.."—cassette tapes, CDs, or books-on-tape to play in the car on the commute home.
- "September Morning"—bamboo garden rake for the fall leaves.

• Request that each guest wear something appropriate as well. For example, "7 a.m." might require robe and slippers, or "July Afternoon" a swimsuit, sun-glasses, and wide-brimmed beach hat. (Encourage the guests to be as creative as possible.)

• Decorate with clocks and calendars, plus clever items pertaining to certain times, days or months, such as beach towels for July or children's valentines for February.

• Create a centerpiece from a decorated cuckoo clock.

• Provide a free Hallmark pocket calendar for each guest as a favor.

Potluck Shower

• The invitations can be written on recipe cards, asking each guest to bring a homemade dish in a container that becomes the gift. If it is a salad luncheon, each guest brings her favorite salad; for a co-ed dinner party, the guests will be asked to bring designated dinner dishes, such as meatballs or scalloped potatoes, or green bean casserole; or for a dessert party, ask your guests to bring their favorite desserts. Be sure the guests understand that, in addition to the food dishes, the serving containers are gifts, along with recipe cards for each dish.

• This is one of the most economical showers you can host because the guests bring the eats.

Christmas in July

Although this party has a Christmas theme, it can be a lot of fun in July, or any other time of year. The object is to give the couple a healthy start toward their supply of Christmas decorations for their home, yard, and Christmas tree.

- If you're one of those organized people who has saved last year's Christmas cards, you can cut them up and glue the pieces to your homemade invitations, name tags or place cards.
- It's easy to decorate for one of these parties. If you've already decorated your home for Christmas, you won't need to add a thing. If the party is in July or any other month except December, you'll need to drag your Christmas boxes out of storage and spread a few things around, including an artificial tree if you have one.
- As the guests arrive, their gifts can be placed under the tree and then, as they are opened, any ornaments or tree trimmings can be displayed on the branches. Give your tree a little help by tying it with ribbons in the bride's wedding colors and wrapping it with garlands of popcorn you have strung in advance.
- If you don't have a tree, the gifts can be stashed in a huge white cloth "Santa's pack" or inside a cardboard box that has been wrapped with Christmas paper.
- Serve Christmas goodies, of course—candy canes, Christmas cookies, or nut bread.

Affordable bridal shower games

Bridal shower scavenger hunt

This "hunt" takes place inside the women's purses. Set the timer for four minutes and see how many of these items each woman can find in her handbag. The guest with the most points wins.

A tip.

- Here's a "swoonable" idea: Have her fiancé arrive during the party as a surprise, presenting her with a long-stemmed rose or a floral bouquet. Not only will the bride be touched by this romantic gesture, but the guests will enjoy seeing the groom-to-be in person.
- See my book, *Complete Book of Wedding Showers,* for more party themes, games, and decorations.

Bridal shower scavenger hunt

Column 1		Column 2	
20 points per item:		**10 points per item:**	
$100 bill	____	Eyelash curler	____
Silver dollar coin	____	Mascara	____
Dental floss	____	Face powder	____
Toothbrush	____	Pain reliever	____
Dictionary	____	Rubber band	____
Smelling salts	____	Tweezers	____
Magnifying glass	____	Nail clippers	____
Nail polish remover	____	Breath mints/spray	____
Cotton swabs	____	Zipper top plastic bag	____
Alarm clock	____	Calculator	____
Pair of gloves	____	Notebook	____
Pocket knife	____	Shopping list	____
Photo of mother	____		
Candy bar	____	**5 points per item:**	
Cigar	____	Lipstick/lip balm	____
Piece of fresh fruit	____	Hair comb	____
Cellular telephone	____	Hand lotion	____
		Nail file/emery board	____
10 points per item:		Regular mirror	____
Postage stamps	____	Tissue	____
Scissors	____	Sun glasses	____
Pencil with an eraser	____	Eye glasses	____
Cloth handkerchief	____	Credit card	____
Address book	____	Photos of children	____
		Chewing gum	____
TOTAL POINTS FROM COLUMN 1 ____		Pen	____
		TOTAL POINTS FROM COLUMN 2 ____	
		TOTAL POINTS FROM COLUMN 1 +____	
		TOTAL ____	

The Mystery Spice Game

Cover the labels on ten different spices, such as sage, ginger, chili powder, cinnamon, nutmeg, curry powder, garlic and thyme. Number them from "1" to "10." Furnish each guest with paper and pencil. Pass the spices around the room, one at a time. The guests must identify the spices by sight and smell (they may not touch or taste them). The guest with the most correct answers wins.

Wedding Rehearsal Dinner

The wedding rehearsal dinner follows the ceremony rehearsal, usually the day before the wedding. It's traditionally hosted and paid for by the groom's parents, although the costs may be shared or paid entirely by the bride's parents, the couple's grandparents, members of the wedding party, or other friends. Fortunately, this dinner is no longer expected to be an elegant, expensive sit-down dinner, but can be an affordable, informal affair. Also, it's the type of get-together where the love shown and sentiments expressed are the most important factors, and they don't cost a dime!

Affordable, informal options

- A barbecue or picnic in a park (depending on the weather and time of year).
- Pizza or spaghetti at the bride's or groom's home.
- A swim party around someone's pool.
- Hot and cold "potluck" dishes served in a room at the rehearsal site.
- "Dutch treat" at a local restaurant where a private room has been reserved.

Of course, if someone wants to pay for an elegant catered dinner, that's fine, too, just as long as there are toasts to the bride and groom, which are the only required element for a rehearsal dinner.

Who should be invited:

Here is a list of the people who should be invited to the rehearsal dinner, in addition to the couple and their parents, of course:

- Members of the wedding party and their spouses or fiancées.
- The wedding coordinator and his or her spouse.
- Parents of any children participating in the wedding. The children themselves, especially if very young, should be left with a babysitter during the dinner.
- Member of the clergy and his or her spouse.
- Special out-of-town relatives, including grandparents.

Note: It's perfectly acceptable to extend invitations for the rehearsal dinner via word-of-mouth, which will save the cost of printed invitations.

A tip. The most important thing when planning the rehearsal dinner is to have a comfortable setting where everyone can relax, visit, and enjoy each other before the big day.

Rehearsal dinner activities

- The host sees that introductions are made all around; this is a wonderful opportunity for the extended families of the bride and groom to meet and get to know each other.
- Various family members may want to tell little stories about the bride and groom when they were young.
- Home videos or slide shows showing the couple as they were growing up are fun.
- If the get-together is quite informal, you may include swimming, mixer games, volleyball or horseshoes—anything to loosen everyone up after the stress of planning the wedding.
- This is also a great time to say "thank-you" to those present who have helped with the wedding preparations and to

give gifts to the members of your wedding party, if you haven't already done so.

• Toasts are the only essential element of a rehearsal dinner, in this order:

- The best man toasts the bride and groom.
- The groom toasts his bride and her parents
- The bride toasts her groom and his parents

After these traditional toasts, anyone may offer one and, by the way, rehearsal dinner toasts are usually more personal and humorous than those at the wedding reception.

Note: See my book, *Complete Book of Wedding Toasts*.

Wedding Receptions

wedding reception traditionally accounts for 30 to 50 percent of the entire cost of the wedding, so if your total wedding budget is $20,000, the average cost of a wedding today, your reception will probably cost between $6,000 and $10,000. So, what are some ways to cut down on the cost of the reception? Here are several of the most popular choices.

Affordable reception venues

- A venue owned by your city, county, or state, such as a park, senior center, natural history museum, rose garden, or a marina. These sites are usually bargain-priced, but they go fast, so the trick is to book them early.
- The backyard of the bride's family home, or that of another friend or family member.
- A room or hall on the grounds of the church or synagogue where your ceremony is taking place, often available for free or at little cost.
- A venue available through your local historical society.
- An alfresco venue, such as one within a national park, on the beach, or alongside a mountain stream.
- A venue available through your local Chamber of Commerce, such as a private mansion, ranch, or retirement community clubhouse.
- Choose a reception site where you have control of the food, beverage, and wedding cake. Many commercial

sites require that you order from their food and beverage menu and order the wedding cake from their pastry chef.

Affordable day and time

- Avoid getting married on a Saturday; try for a Friday evening instead.
- Avoid the month of June.
- Plan a morning wedding, which will tend to cost less in every way than an afternoon or evening wedding.

Affordable decorations

- Borrow white lace tablecloths for the serving tables.
- Decorate with affordable balloons, acetate ribbons, and inexpensive tulle netting.
- Let the ceremony flowers serve double-duty for the reception. For example, any free-standing arrangements can be brought from the ceremony site to the reception site and placed on the serving tables or beside the cake table. Also, the bridesmaids' bouquets can serve to decorate the bride and groom's table.
- If you find a venue that is affordable, but leaves a little to be desired in its ambience, have the reception at night with only tiny white Christmas lights and tall white candles to give it a romantic glow.
- If you have an outdoor reception venue, you may not need much in the way of decorations.
- Rent or borrow decorations, furniture, or accessories, according to your wedding reception theme. For example, potted silk ficus trees and plants, white picket fence, portable gazebo, tiki torches, strings of tiny white Christmas lights, wrought iron or wooden benches, patio tables and umbrellas, wreaths, trellises, wicker lawn furniture, and so forth.

Note: By giving your wedding reception theme just a little thought ahead of time, you can choose one that's not only clever, but affordable to put together.

Affordable reception food and drink

- As I mentioned previously, it's important for you to have control of the food and drink, which means reserving a venue that allows you to bring in your own caterer or provide your own food dishes and beverages.
- Certain times of day require less expensive food service. For example, a morning wedding (before 11 a.m.) may only require a light continental or buffet breakfast. A midday wedding (11 a.m. to 1 p.m.) only requires a light luncheon buffet, and an afternoon wedding (1 p.m. to 4 p.m.) will only require a light appetizer buffet, along with wedding cake and toasting beverage.
- Provide your own choice of food dishes, purchased from a deli or discount food supplier, along with home-cooked side dishes donated by friends and family members.
- Dress up your table with borrowed china, silver, and crystal. As they say, "It's all in the presentation." So, with the use of elegant tablecloths and serving pieces, along with a few lace doilies, you can give your table an elegant presentation, in spite of the affordable foods to be served.
- In lieu of on-demand champagne service or an open bar, opt instead for a couple bowls of inexpensive fruit-flavored wedding punch, one spiked with champagne and one not.
- Cut down on the cost of the wedding cake by providing a "dummy cake," along with sheet cakes that have been baked ahead by family members; or by ordering from a private individual who makes them in her own home; or by purchasing a small, affordable wedding cake, supplemented with homemade side cakes served out of the kitchen. Another popular alternative to the full-priced commercial bakery cake is to order through your supermarket bakery, where you'll find amazing cakes for the money.

    Note: A "dummy cake" is one made with Styrofoam layers that have been frosted and decorated with fresh flowers and your own cake topper (similar to the ones you see on display in bakery windows.)

- See my book, *How to Have a Big Wedding on a Small Budget, 3rd Edition*, that includes hundreds of cost-cutting ideas, including specific wedding reception menus and per-item costs.
- See my book, *Beautiful Wedding Decorations & Gifts on a Small Budget*, for more decorating ideas, including detailed instructions for tying a tulle bow, decorating with balloons, and creating inexpensive cake toppers.
- See my book, *Complete Book of Wedding Toasts*, for toasts that should be offered during the reception.

Affordable reception music

- Enlist the services of an amateur or professional DJ, instead of hiring a six-piece band.
- Take advantage of your talented friends and family members: Ask them if they would provide free recitals as their wedding gifts to you.
- Search out reasonably priced musicians to play at your reception. For example, there are university music majors who relish the chance to perform. Call the chairman of your local university music department or ask recent brides and grooms for suggestions.
- Create a series of one-hour cassette tapes with music of your own choice. Number the tapes so that someone you trust can begin each tape on cue. For example, Tape Number One may contain music to be played during the food service. Tape Number Two may contain the dance music, beginning with your first dance, and so forth. It takes a lot of work ahead of time to pull this off, but you'll save hundreds, if not thousands, of dollars, plus you'll be in total control of which music is played when.

Baby Showers

baby shower is usually scheduled a month or so before the baby is due, or it may follow the baby's christening or baptism, or it can be a "welcome to the family" celebration on the day Mommy and baby arrive home from the hospital. The nice thing about any modern baby shower is that there are no strict rules to follow, and it may be hosted by anyone—friend, relative, or co-worker. Here is a selection of affordable baby shower themes.

Family Heirloom Shower

- This is a party attended by the female family members: mothers, aunts, great-aunts, grandmothers, great-grandmothers, and so forth. The theme of the party is to pass down family heirlooms or antiques in honor of the new baby.

    The type of heirlooms often passed down from generation to generation include:
    - Christening dress.
    - Hand-knitted or crocheted blanket.
    - Silver baby spoon.
    - Silver hair brush.
    - Music box.
    - Silver haircut box (to hold hair from first haircut).
    - Silver tooth-fairy box.
    - Silver or porcelain picture frames.
- Use a "Family Tree" as the theme of your decorations: Cut them out of construction paper or poster board for invitations and name tags, and decorate a silk ficus tree

133

with photos of each family member, plus a miniature cradle that says, "Baby Simpson" or the name of the expected baby if it has been decided.

- Transfer old family photos and home movies onto a videotape that can be shown as entertainment. Try to find photos and movies of family members when they were young, including those of the expectant parents.

Choo-Choo Train Party

- Cut construction paper or poster board into caboose shapes to use as invitations, name tags, or place cards.
- An electric train can serve as the table centerpiece, or it can run on tracks that have been creatively placed around the platters of food on a buffet table.
- Using yarn, connect boxes of animal crackers together to form trains; set them at each place setting as party favors.

Tip: Wear an engineer's cap and use a wooden train whistle as you conduct the games.

Time-of-Day Shower

- Ask each guest to bring a gift to be used a certain time of day. For example:

Bath time (9 a.m.)	Bath thermometer
Lunch time (Noon)	Tipper cup
Nap time (2 p.m.)	Sleepers
Play time (4 p.m.)	Stuffed animals

- A grandfather's clock can serve as the main party decoration. Decorate it with ribbons and baby-related items.

Pamper Mommy Party

- This is a special party designed to honor and pamper the Mommy-to-be.
- Make her feel beautiful with a free makeover, complements of your favorite cosmetics representative; a fresh

new hair style, complements of a professional hair stylist; and to-die-for nails, complements of a professional manicurist.
* The gifts for this party are for Mommy: a lacy, feminine nightie; satin robe and slippers; bed jacket; bubble bath; lotions; perfume; or a "hospital basket" filled with books, magazines, candy, and so on.

Fill-the-Freezer Shower

* A good idea for the mother who's expecting her second or third child, because she probably has the basics and what she *really* needs is some relief during the first two or three weeks after the baby is born. So, what could be better than to furnish her with frozen homemade casseroles, desserts, breads, and so forth?
* In addition to the frozen dishes, the guests furnish corresponding recipe cards that are placed in a recipe box to be given to the expectant mother.

Everyone's expecting

This is a tongue-in-cheek type of party where all the guests arrive *quite* pregnant. The idea is that "we sympathize with you, because we're all going through the same thing." Keep the idea a secret: it should be a surprise to the expectant mother.

Tip: Suggest that the guests wear big shirts or borrowed maternity clothes over their puffy-pillow tummies. Give prizes for "The Funniest," "Most Creative," and so on.

Gift displays

Although gifts can be set on a table in the corner of the room, it's much nicer to display them in a special way, creating a focal point as the guests arrive. Here are a few affordable ideas:
* An enormous golf umbrella covered with satin fabric and ribbons and set on the floor to "protect" the gifts from the "elements."
* A decorated plastic or wicker laundry basket.
* A decorated child's red wagon.

Tip: After the gifts have been opened, display them on a clothesline that has been suspended across the room. Use colorful plastic clothespins to attach gifts to the clothesline.

Baby Shower Invitations

Baby Diapers

Cut triangular pieces from stationery, construction paper, or fabric. Fold into a tri-fold diaper, fastening with a safety pin or diaper pin.

Customized Hospital Bracelets

Make your own hospital bracelets (like the one attached to the baby's wrist). Cut white poster board into strips. Print the party invitation on both sides of each strip, cover with clear Contact paper, and form into a bracelet by stapling or taping ends together.

Plastic Baby Bib

Bibs can be used as invitations by writing the information across the front with marking pens. Fold and enclose in envelopes.

Baby Shower Games

Mystery Baby Food Game

Preparation:
- 10 jars of baby food
- Paper and pencil for each guest
- One small plastic spoon per guest

Cover the labels on 10 jars of baby food, such as pears, squash, sweet potatoes, or bananas. Number them from "1" to "10." Furnish each guest with paper, pencil, and a small, plastic spoon. Pass the jars around the room, one at a time. The guests must identify the food by sight, smell and taste. (Each guest is instructed to dip the tip of her spoon into the food). The guest with the most correct answers wins.

Tip: If you really want to make this game challenging, add a few of the new "gourmet" baby food mixtures, such as Apples & Chicken, Pear & Wild Blueberry, or Chicken & Rice.

The baby name game

Preparation:
- Duplicate the list below, one per guest
- One pen or pencil per guest
- A timer

Set the timer for 10 minutes. The guest who matches the most names with their correct meanings wins a prize.

_____	Erin	1.	Graceful
_____	Trevor	2.	Gift of the Lord
_____	Darren	3.	Honey Bee
_____	Casey	4.	Pretty
_____	Matthew	5.	Peace
_____	Linda	6.	Prudent
_____	Ann	7.	Brave
_____	Jason	8.	Grounds Keeper
_____	Garth	9.	Great
_____	Melissa	10.	Healer

Answers:
5. Erin—Peace
6. Trevor—Prudent
9. Darren—Great
7. Casey—Brave
2. Matthew—Gift of the Lord
4. Linda—Pretty
1. Ann—Graceful
10. Jason—Healer
8. Garth—Grounds Keeper
3. Melissa—Honey Bee

Baby word scramble

Preparation:
- Duplicate the list below, one per guest
- One pen or pencil per guest
- A timer

Here is a list of words for your guests to unscramble. Make as many copies as you need. They all have to do with babies. See who can unscramble the most words in three minutes.

A tip.

- First-time grandparents appreciate a baby shower planned especially for them, furnishing their home with "baby sitting" toys and supplies.
- Here's an outstanding "small budget" idea: If the baby shower is being given after the baby has been born, present the parents with a free card of congratulations signed by the President of the United States. Send the baby's name, birth date, and address to: The White House Greeting Office, Room 39, Washington, D.C. 20500
- See my book, *Complete Book of Baby Showers*, for more party themes and ideas for invitations, name tags, decorating, party menus, games, and gift suggestions.

1. YBBA TLOBET   _____
2. SARIPED   _____
3. IRCB   _____
4. TLYEATE   _____
5. LRDAEC   _____
6. RLUMFAO   _____
7. IGRNKCO HRCIA   _____
8. KLEBTNA   _____
9. TELTAR   _____
10. CRIPEIAF   _____

(Answers: baby bottle; diapers; crib; layette; cradle; formula; rocking chair; blanket; rattle; pacifier)

Wedding Anniversary Celebrations

I t's appropriate to celebrate every wedding anniversary; however, early anniversaries are often hosted by the couple themselves; later anniversaries, such as the 25th, 40th, and 50th, are almost always hosted by the couple's children, or if they have no children, by close friends. Here are affordable ways to host one of these affairs.

Invitations

Scan the couple's wedding photo onto the front of a computer-generated invitation, or have copies made and glue them to the front of a home-lettered card. These invitations may be mailed or hand-delivered.

Decorations

- Borrow decorating ideas from Chapter 32.
- Decorate with the couple's wedding photos, a display of the wedding gown, plus any other memorabilia from their wedding.
- A 25th anniversary celebration is known as the "silver anniversary," so silver ribbons and balloons are in order.
- For a 50th anniversary celebration, the color scheme is usually gold and white.

Fun Stuff

- If a formal celebration, it is appropriate to form a receiving line, in this order:

1. Host and/or hostess stands first in the line.
2. The honored couple (framed by their original maid of honor and best man, if in attendance).
3. The couple's children.

- If available, play the couple's original wedding video.
- Provide a wedding arch for the couple to stand under as they greet their guests and have photos taken.
- In the case of a 50th wedding anniversary, present the couple with a special anniversary greeting from the President of the United States. Write The White House, Greetings Office, Room 39, 1600 Pennsylvania Avenue NW, Washington, D.C. 20500-1600. A couple must be married 50 or more years to be entitled to this impressive greeting from the President.
- If it is an informal party, a perfect game to play is the "Newlywed Game/Oldywed Game" (see Chapter 4).
- Play recorded wedding music during the party.
- Videotape the activities, and play it back near the end of the party.
- A poignant moment may be the renewal of the wedding vows. The couple may repeat the actual vows they recited on their wedding day, or they may decide to recite personalized vows composed especially for the occasion. In my book, *Complete Book of Wedding Vows*, you will find more than 30 versions of "Reaffirmation Vows." Here are three examples. The first two are free-style, personalized versions, and the third is formal, from the classical writings of Walt Whitman:

"_____, thank you for your love and your faithfulness to me all these years. It's easy to love someone at first, when we look our best, say the right things, and are always on our best behavior; but you have seen me at my absolute worst, and still you love me, which makes me love you all the more. Thank you for always being there for me, in every way, and thank you for all you will be to me in the years to come. I pledge again to you this day to love you for the rest of our days."

"On this day, _____ years ago, I promised to love you and cherish you all the days of my life. I hereby reaffirm that promise, in the presence of God and our family. _____, you have been my friend and companion and the revered mother/father of our children, but most of all you have been my beautiful loving bride (or handsome loving husband) for all these years, and I renew my pledge of eternal devotion to you this day."

"I give you my hand!
I give you my love more precious than money,
I give you myself before preaching or law;
Will you give me yourself? Will you come travel with me?
Shall we stick by each other as long as we live?"
—Walt Whitman, from "Song of the Open Road"

 **A tip.** See my book, *Complete Book of Wedding Toasts*, for wedding anniversary toasts.

Party Fare

- Depending on the formality of the celebration, the party fare can be anything from a family picnic in the park, to a potluck buffet dinner, to a formal sit-down dinner (see affordable menu ideas in Chapter 44).
- Two musts for any wedding anniversary celebration, however, are a wedding cake and champagne for toasting.
- If it's the first wedding anniversary, it's customary to resurrect the top layer of the wedding cake from the freezer, to be cut by and served to the couple, in addition to a larger cake to be served to all the guests.

Retirement Party

A retirement party doesn't need to be an elaborate affair to accomplish its purpose: honoring the retiree. The fact that you've put together a little celebration is what counts. Of course, if you have several co-hosts, the party can be even bigger and better than originally planned.

Invitations

Depending on the party's theme, you can create invitations from travel brochures; time cards from the retiree's place of business; or computer-generated invitations attached to a small object relating to his hobby or interests. For example, tie the invitation to a miniature fishing pole made from a twig, string, and a big rubber worm; place inside a tiny "cookbook" made from poster board "cover" and paper "pages"; or attach to a miniature golf club or a sack of golf tees. Another option: Create "Do Not Disturb" signs (the type usually hung on a hotel doorknob) and print the invitation on the back side of the sign.

Decorations

- Computer-generate a "congratulations" banner to display on the wall behind your serving table, or use tempera paint on a banner made from colored butcher paper.
- Decorate around your honored guest's hobbies or goals. For example, if he plans on spending a lot of time fishing, drag out your fishing gear and use it to decorate the room. Or, if her goal is to take a cruise, borrow cruise brochures and posters from your friendly travel agent.

- Decorate with a "year-at-a-glance" calendar (available at any office supply store), with dates filled in with humorous activities, such as "1 to 3:30 p.m.—afternoon nap," "Watch bocce at the park," and so forth.
- Borrow wooden rocking chairs from everyone you know and set them around the room.
- Ask the guests to decorate the party venue by wearing attire appropriate to the theme. For example, if the party has a "Gone Fishin'" theme, the guests can wear their fishing clothes and carry fishing poles; for a gardening theme, they can wear their work grubbies and carry rakes and hoes.

Fun Stuff

- A "Roast" or a "This Is Your Life" presentation may be in order (see Chapter 4).
- Toasts are a must for any retirement party.

If gifts are in order, there are many clever retirement gifts available, or suggest gifts appropriate to the retiree's hobbies, goals, upcoming trips, and so forth.

Party Fare

- If you're co-hosting the party, you may be able to afford a light luncheon buffet.
- Serve appetizers and light snacks (see Chapter 44), along with a congratulatory cake.
- It can be a dessert-only party.
- Be sure to serve some kind of toasting beverage, if only inexpensive sparkling cider.

Hawaiian Luau

A luau is one of the most popular party themes in the country today. Fortunately, it's a "hang-loose" type of party that can be hosted on a budget. Plus, it's a refreshing escape from reality, something we all need these days. It's also one of those parties where your guests' party attire adds greatly to the party ambience.

Invitations

Collect Hawaiian travel brochures from your friendly neighborhood travel agency; attach a hand-made or computer-generated invitation. Send through the mail or hand-deliver to save on postage. Be sure to ask the guests to dress Hawaiian for the party. If the party will take place around a swimming pool, ask the guests to also bring their swimming attire.

Costumes

- Grass skirts and halter tops.
- Hawaiian shirts/sarongs/muumuus.
- Colorful leis, beads or shell necklaces.
- Bare feet.
- Flowers in the women's hair.

Decorations

Whether your party is held outdoors, which is ideal, or indoors due to inclement weather, here are some popular decorating ideas.

- Cover the walls with brochures and travel posters of Hawaii.
- Hang fishnets from the ceiling or over doorways.
- Create displays of sand, seashells, and driftwood using a sack of ordinary sandbox sand.
- Fill the room or patio with live or silk plants that are as "tropical looking" as possible.
- Set arrangements of large, colorful fresh or silk flowers around the room.
- If the party will be held outdoors, borrow all the tiki torches you can from your friends and family members.
- Use large round fish bowls as centerpieces with live gold fish. If you can borrow the fish bowls, the gold fish can be purchased inexpensively from your local pet store.
- If you have a swimming pool, float a rubber raft filled with colorful silk or fresh flowers and lighted votive candles.
- Wrap galvanized buckets of iced drinks with grass hula skirts.

Fun Stuff

- Play Hawaiian background music throughout the party.
- Greet your guests as they arrive by draping inexpensive plastic leis around their necks and kissing each guest on the cheek.
- If the party takes place around a pool, include swimming as an activity.
- Hold a hula contest. Purchase inexpensive hula skirts from your favorite import store, or make them with strips of green crepe paper or plastic garbage bags. Tie skirts around a few of the guests (be sure to include the men), play recorded Hawaiian music, and see how well they can hula. (Keep your camera or videocam ready!)
- Hula lessons, whether amateur or professional, are always popular.
- Provide each guest with a length of flowered Hawaiian fabric, plus scissors and safety pins. Set a timer and see who can come up with the cleverest Hawaiian garment in five minutes. They can use the fabric to make a scarf, headband, belt, hat, halter top, or short sarong skirt, among other garments.

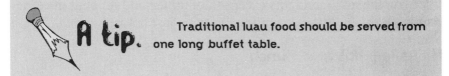

A tip. Traditional luau food should be served from one long buffet table.

- Ask a talented male "lip-syncer" to practice ahead of time "singing" to Don Ho's recordings of *Tiny Bubbles* and *Pearly Shells*. This is really effective, especially if he can stay in sync with Don Ho.

Party Fare

- Serve an inexpensive version of an authentic Hawaiian luau menu:
  - Roast pork, beef, or grilled fish, whichever is in season and on sale.
  - Canned pineapple slices, soaked in teriyaki sauce and lightly grilled.
  - Fresh strawberries or melons, depending on seasonal prices.
  - Sweet Hawaiian bread.
  - Canned yams or sweet potatoes, baked with brown sugar.
  - Fresh green salad with tomatoes, onions, raw zucchini, cucumbers, or any other raw vegetables.
  - Roasted bananas and hawaiian fruit salad (see the following recipes).

Roasted bananas

Peel, dip in melted butter and sprinkle with sugar; wrap in aluminum foil and roast for 20 minutes; serve with a drizzle of rum). Bananas are almost always plentiful and affordable, so serve plenty.

Hawaiian fruit salad

- 1 cup pineapple tidbits, drained
- 1 1/2 cup Mandarin oranges, drained
- 1 1/2 cup miniature marshmallows
- 1 cup inexpensive mayonnaise with a little pineapple juice and sugar whipped in
- Freshly ground nutmeg

Combine all ingredients except the nutmeg and let chill in refrigerator overnight. Sprinkle with the nutmeg just before serving.

Hawaiian Volcano Punch

Fill a punch bowl with fruit punch or inexpensive powdered fruit drink, scoops of raspberry sherbet, and cold raspberry soda or ginger ale poured over the sherbet, which will foam, creating a "volcano."

Tailgate Party

The idea of a tailgate party is to get together with a bunch of friends who already plan to attend a certain concert or sports event; arrive early and eat in the parking lot before the big event. One of these parties can be fun and affordable; it just takes a little planning.

Invitations

This is a casual get-together; invite everyone over the telephone, via e-mail, or by sending a fax.

Decorations

A tailgate party provides its own "decorations," but if you want to follow the trend you can go all out by dressing it up tongue-in-cheek with candlesticks, silver serving trays and utensils, crystal wine glasses, white linen tablecloths, bouquets of flowers, and so forth.

Fun Stuff

Bring a boom box and tapes or CDs, or a portable TV to watch pre-game coverage. Actually, the idea of eating out of your trunk in a parking lot provides its own fun.

Party Fare

The key to affordable party fare is for everyone involved to contribute to the eats, including a side dish and meat. That will

A tip.

- A few TV trays will come in handy.
- Bring plenty of utensils: barbecue tools, bottle opener, sharp carving knife, steak knives, serving forks and spoons, napkins, and paper towels.
- Bring several garbage bags; it makes the cleanup a lot easier.

cut down on the cost considerably, so that your main concern will be to furnish the condiments, blankets, lawn chairs, utensils, bottle opener, tablecloths, napkins, and so forth.

- Set up your portable barbecue to cook hamburgers, hot dogs, roasted potatoes, or corn on the cob.
- Bring heroes or cold-cut sandwiches.
- Bring an ice chest filled with fried chicken, macaroni salad, cold veggies and dips, cheeses, beer, and soda.
- Serve potato chips and cookies and bring insulated containers of hot coffee or hot chocolate, depending on the weather.
- Don't forget the condiments: catsup, mustard, mayo, relish, pickles, olives, butter, cream, sugar, salt, and pepper.

Video
Scavenger Hunt

As many of you may already know if you've read any of my other party books, this is one of my favorite parties, not only to host, but to attend. And, best of all, it's really affordable—one of the biggest party bangs for the buck!

The idea is to divide the guests into groups of four to six people each (enough to fill one car.) The groups compete against each other to see which one can return first having videotaped every required scene or stunt on the scavenger hunt list.

You will need to provide one fully-charged video camera and tape per group, along with the list of required scenes and stunts. Fortunately, most of the guests will be able to come up with their own camera and videotape.

Invitations

Have copies made of an enlarged photo of a humorous stunt or scene; write the invitation on the back of each and mail or hand-deliver. Ask the guests to wear casual, comfortable clothing that will allow them to perform the stunts required.

Decorations

- Set up folding chairs "theater style" in front of your TV.
- Tie balloon bouquets to a couple of the chairs.
- Decorate your Ice Cream Sundae Bar with balloons, colorful plastic bowls, and napkins.

151

Fun stuff

You can come up with any scenes or stunts you would like, but to give you an idea of what seems to work, here are a few of the stunts that have been required at some recent Video Scavenger Hunt parties:

- One of the members of the group standing in front of (or sitting on) a statue.
- Several members of the group joining a street entertainer in his or her act.
- A stranger singing the national anthem.
- One or more members of a group standing under a public clock at an exact time (such as 7:21 p.m.).
- A member of the group singing a 1970s' song on a stage.
- A member of the group singing "I Wish I Were an Oscar Meyer Weiner" while standing in the hot dog section of a local grocery store.
- A member of the group standing on a surfboard.
- Any stranger from the state of _____(name any state you would like other than your own).
- Members of the group standing in front of a lighted outdoor Christmas tree, or waving an American Flag, or "offering" candy from a box of Valentine's candy, or carrying an Easter basket while "pretending" to search for Easter eggs, and so on. (These stunts depend on the season of the year.)
- Go to the home of a friend or acquaintance, "abduct" the person, and bring him or her back to the party with you.
- Carrying a stranger's groceries to her car.
- A stranger trying to spell potato (or any other word you would like).
- Opening a store door for a stranger while asking for a tip.
- Asking a stranger to recite the names of all the continents.
- One or more members of the group singing at a karaoke bar.
- A couple dancing to department store or elevator music (*in* the store or elevator!).
- Read a book or recite a poem to a stranger.
- Go to a department store and try on a shirt or dress that is several sizes too small; then ask the clerk if she thinks it fits.
- Any stranger who has skied at Vail, Colorado; or been to Epcot Center; or ridden the subway in New York City (or anything appropriate to your part of the country).

- A stranger demonstrating the Macarena.
- Find a stranger named "Bob."
- Find a stranger who knows your state flower.
- Find a stranger who can imitate John Wayne.
- A policeman drawing a chalk line on the ground around one of the members of your group.
- Go up to a stranger at a service station, fill his car with gas, wash his windows, and check his oil.
- Stand beside a tombstone.
- Sit on a fire truck with a fireman.
- "Road kill" (an animal that has been run over on the highway).
- Stand by the greeter at Wal-Mart and greet the customers.
- Go to a hardware store and get a clerk to explain the difference between a flat head and a Phillips screw driver.
- Spell a certain word with your bodies while standing in front of a library.
- Wash dishes at a restaurant.
- Sing an Elvis song while standing under a neon sign.
- Hold a chicken.

These are examples of the types of stunts you'll need to add to your list, but I'm sure you can come up with dozens more of your own. The list should contain no more than 15 or 20 stunts total because each carload will be given only an hour and a half to videotape as many as they can. The guests are given an exact time they must return to the party venue. For example, if they leave at 7 p.m. they must return by 8:30 p.m. If not back on time, the group is disqualified.

Once everyone has returned, the videotapes are played back, with each stunt scored by all the guests present on a point system from "1" to "3":

1: Videotaped the stunt, whether it was done well or not.
2: The stunt showed some creativity.
3: The stunt was *exceptionally* creative.

Five bonus points are given to a group if they came up with an original stunt of their own. For example, at one party a big husky man went into a Wal Mart store and stood in the aisle while trying on bras, as the other members of the group *seriously* critiqued the way each one fit.

The team with the most total points wins.

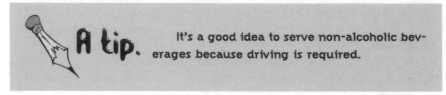

A tip. It's a good idea to serve non-alcoholic beverages because driving is required.

Party Fare

- Serve snacks, appetizers, and cold or hot beverages before the hunt, while the guests are waiting for everyone to arrive and the game rules are being explained.
- Serve do-it-yourself ice cream sundaes while everyone is watching the videos after the hunt.

Casual Lunch or Dinner Parties

A casual luncheon or dinner party is easy to put together on a small budget; you just need to be careful with the selection of your menu. As we already know it's all in the presentation.

Invitations

Send an informal invitation, such as a hand-written note, or simply give your guests a call.

Decorations

All you'll need for a casual dinner is a cleverly set table (see Chapter 2). Remember that it's possible to create a charming ambience without spending a dime.

Fun Stuff

- Play easy-listening background music during the meal, but keep the volume low enough to enjoy the pleasant conversation.
- After the meal, you have the option of playing one or two of the games included in Chapter 4.

Party Fare

Serve your own affordable tried-and-true favorites, or put a meal together from the recipes found in Chapter 44, such as:

- If you're planning on inviting more than eight guests, you may want to serve the meal buffet-style, which is the easiest way to serve a large crowd, especially if you don't have any help.
- A "potluck" meal (where each guest brings a dish) makes for extra-easy entertaining, because you have the fun of getting together without all the work. Of course, it also cuts down on the costs as well.

- One or two salads, hot Reuben sandwiches, and appleberry crunch.
- Italian pasta bar, tossed green salad, hot garlic bread, and raspberry lemon trifle.
- Swedish meatballs, hot potato casserole, fruit balls, and Swedish macaroon tea cakes.
- Tijuana Tamale Pie, chips and salsa, Taco Salad, and ice cream sundaes.
- Hamburger pie, tossed green salad, garlic bread, and baked Alaska.

Cruise Ship Formal Night Dinner Party

A cruise ship formal night dinner is a way to present formal cuisine in a novel way. The idea is to overwhelm your guests with the party's theme so they don't notice that your "formal cuisine" is actually composed of affordable food dishes presented in an elegant way. In other words, you'll be converting ordinary, inexpensive groceries into exotic dishes with French names.

Of course, by the time you add the formal attire, formal table settings, and romantic ambience, you will have pulled off an incredible coup: an elegant formal dinner party without the traditional expense.

This party is great fun to put together, especially if you've been on a cruise or two and enjoyed their traditional formal nights.

Invitations

You can't go "on board" without a "Boarding Pass," so create invitations that resemble official boarding passes. Print the invitations onto sheets of heavy 8-1/2" x 11" paper, with three invitations per sheet (each will be approximately 3-1/3" x 8-1/2"). The suggested invitation is on the next page.

Option: You may attach a cruiseline brochure to each boarding pass (visit your friendly travel agent.)

Attire

This is a formal affair, so as hosts you should be dressed for the occasion in tuxedo or dark suit and evening gown.

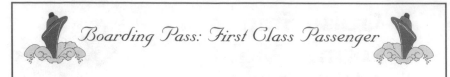

Boarding Pass: First Class Passenger

_____

Name of invited guest(s)

S. S. Whittaker (use your last name)

Departs from port: *your address*

On: *date*

At: *time*

You will be a guest for dinner at the Captain's table

Formal Attire Requested

RSVP: Cruise Director, _____**, at** (tele. #)

Decorations

- Post a cruiseline travel poster at the end of your driveway, followed by the words "[YOUR NAME] Harbor Ahead." Create a "gangplank" by roping off your front walkway into the house.
- Hang a large banner over your front door that says: **WELCOME ABOARD.**
- Use silver-colored poster board to create "portholes" to be hung on the walls of your dining room: Cut poster board in large circles, framed by "bolted" frame, with water and sky painted inside the frame.
- Hang life preservers around the room, with the ship's name (see "Fun Stuff"). Tie a piece of rope around each preserver. (If you can't round up life preservers, use inexpensive Styrofoam rings instead).
- Create an elegant, formal dinner ambience by turning the lights low, lighting candles, and using your best linen tablecloths, silverware, china, and crystal. Add candles and a floral centerpiece, or a less expensive centerpiece of table art (see Chapter 2).

- Use non-toxic markers to decorate the outside edges of the dinner plates with the cruiseline's name and logo.
- Add two or three free-standing, framed dinner menus to the table (see Party Fare).
- Use your calligraphy pen or fancy font on your computer to create elegant place cards for your guests.

Fun Stuff

- As soon as your guests arrive, take them to the "photography studio" for their formal night cruise photos. Set up a solid colored or cruise-appropriate background, if you have access to a cruise poster or ocean scene. Ask each guest to pose holding a ship's life preserver, such as **S. S. Whittaker** (according to the host's last name or the first name of the honored guest, if applicable). Take instant photos of each couple or individual, which are placed on a "display board" during the dinner (just like they do on a cruise ship), then given to the guests to take home as mementos of their "big night."
- Play relaxing classical or semi-classical background music during the dinner conversation. Play loud, rousing march music during the Baked Alaska presentation, such as the last part of Tchaikovsky's "1812 Overture" or any John Phillip Sousa march.

 A tip.

- When your guests call to RSVP, remind them about the requested formal attire; you don't want any guest to arrive in slacks and a sweater because he or she didn't read the invitation carefully!
- Don't rush the meal. One of the most charming qualities of a cruise ship formal dinner is its nice, slow pace. There should be "air" between the courses, giving the guests time to breathe and enjoy pleasant conversation. In other words, drag it out and "milk it" for all its worth!

Party Fare

- This is a "cruise ship formal night," so each dish is given a French name and presented with great fanfare.
- All the recipes for this formal dinner are included in Chapter 44.
- The evening's fare is presented in French to the guests with the framed, calligraphied menus standing on each table. The affordable dishes are given flowery French names and printed on parchment, which is cut to fit any existing, free-standing silver or crystal frames you have available or can borrow for the evening.
- The "French Menu" is to be printed on parchment; you can clue your guests in on the English translations as the dinner goes along, if you like. (You can see an ornate example on the facing page.)
- Here is the English version:
  - Parmesan Mushroom Appetizers
  - Potato Soup
  - Baby Spinach Mandarin Salad
  - Chicken in Wine
  - Cheese Stuffed Tomatoes
  - Asparagus Tips with Hollandaise Sauce
  - Baguettes with Garlic
  - Baked Alaska**
  - Dessert Cheeses
  - After-dinner mints
- A formal dinner party usually requires the serving of alcoholic or non-alcoholic champagne, sparkling cider, or an affordable wine. It's a nice touch to provide a silver ice bucket to keep the bottle chilled; tie the bottle at the neck with a white linen napkin.
- Serve a specialty coffee with the Baked Alaska (see Chapter 42).

** The Baked Alaska is the coup de grace of the evening and is presented with great pomp: turn off the lights, turn on the loud march music, light the sparklers or tall tapered candles on top of the dessert and march around the room several times to the music. Finally, after you've "marched" as much as you dare before the ice cream melts, set the thing down on the table, turn on the lights and serve in chilled bowls.

Sample Ornate French Menu

Champignons á la milanaise

Vichyssoise

Saladé epinards á l'orange

Coq au vin

Tomates farcies au fromage

Pointes d'asperges sauce hollandaise

Pain grillé a l'ail

Surprise du Vésuve

Fromages

Entremets

Dessert Parties

A dessert party is one of the easiest parties to host because, instead of a full meal, all you need to serve is dessert and coffee. A dessert party is also versatile. It can be dressed "up" or "down," depending on its formality; you can serve one dessert or several; and you can add a little entertainment, or just enjoy each other's company.

Invitations

If the party is formal, mail formal computer-generated or calligraphied invitations. If informal, simply pick up the phone and ask, "Would you and Bill like to come over for dessert and coffee Friday night?"

Decorations

As I mentioned, you can dress your party "up" or "down" (see Chapter 2 for "Table Art" suggestions.) For example, if you're hosting a formal, sit-down dessert and coffee party, you can create a romantic ambience by turning off most of the lights in the room and decorating with candles, fresh roses, antique lace, swirling tulle netting, delicate satin ribbons, and tiny white Christmas tree lights.

Fun Stuff

For a formal dessert party, you may want to limit the entertainment to soft background music and good conversation. For an informal dessert party, such as a casual dessert buffet, you can include a couple of games (see Chapter 4).

Part

5

Small-Budget Party Recipes

Did I ever have fun putting this section together! I picked the brains of clever hosts and hostesses across the country for small-budget recipes that are not only creative, but tasty as well. Included here are great small-budget beverages, snacks, and appetizers, plus awesome children's party recipes, as well as teen and adult fare.

If you're like I am, you'll probably like these economical dishes well enough to include them in your day-to-day menus. After all, your family enjoys something a little special from time to time, from a festive dessert to a clever new snack or an eye-catching main dish.

And the beauty of it all is this: These recipes are affordable.

Small Budget Beverages

his chapter contains small-budget beverage recipes for children and adult parties. As you may already know, it's easy to get carried away with party drinks; even smoothies and specialty coffee drinks can add up. So, here are popular, yet economical, party drink recipes.

Non-alcoholic Beverages

- Milk shakes.
- Root beer floats.
- Hot chocolate with marshmallows and whipped cream.
- Hot cider served in mugs with cinnamon sticks.
- Fruit Bubbly (recipe follows).
- Elegant Party Punch (recipe follows).
- Cranberry Punch (recipe follows on the next page).
- Kids' Colada (recipe follows on the next page).

Fruit Bubbly

Freeze fruit juices in ice cube trays. Place two or three in a plastic champagne glass and fill the glass with chilled ginger ale. The drink will bubble as the ice cubes dissolve.

Elegant Party Punch

- 1 can pre-sweetened Kool-Aid (makes 8 quarts)
- 1/2 gallon frozen sherbet (orange, lime, or raspberry)
- 1 bottle (2 liters) generic lemon-lime, raspberry, or orange soda

167

Chill mixed Kool-Aid and lemon-lime soda in advance. Pour Kool-Aid into punch bowl. Add frozen sherbet, using an ice cream scoop. Pour lemon-lime soda over sherbet, which creates an elegant, foamy punch.

Note: If you want an orange punch (for Halloween), combine orange Kool-Aid, orange sherbet, and orange soda. For a green punch, use lime Kool-Aid, lime sherbet, and lemon-lime soda. For a red punch, use any red Kool-Aid, raspberry sherbet, and raspberry soda.

Cranberry Punch

- 5 tea bags
- 5 cups boiling water
- 1/2 teaspoon allspice
- 1/2 teaspoon cinnamon
- 1/2 teaspoon nutmeg
- 1 cup sugar
- 1 quart cranberry juice cocktail
- 3 cups water
- 1 cup orange juice
- 3/4 cup lemon juice

Pour boiling water over tea bags and the spices and steep for 5 minutes. Strain, add sugar, and let cool. Add cranberry juice cocktail, water, orange and lemon juice, and mix. Pour into punch bowl with ice cubes made from lemon juice. Float thin lemon slices on top of the punch.

Kids' Colada

Mix four cups lime sherbet in blender with one cup whole milk; blend until smooth and frothy. Serve in plastic champagne glasses; top with squirt of whipped cream and a cherry.

Specialty Coffee Drinks

Cafe Mocha

Equal amounts of coffee and hot chocolate topped with whipped cream.

Caffe Borgia

Equal amounts of espresso and hot chocolate, served in a demitasse cup, topped with whipped cream and grated orange peel.

Coffee a la Mode

Add two tablespoons vanilla or coffee ice cream to the coffee just before you serve it.

Alcoholic Beverages

Sangria Punch

- 1 gallon red wine
- 4 oranges, sliced and quartered
- 4 apples, peeled, cored and sliced
- 1/2 lemon, sliced
- 1-1/2 cups sugar
- 2 tablespoons cinnamon
- 1 cup light rum

Mix ingredients together in a large crock, glass, or plastic container and store overnight in a cool place. Do not refrigerate. Just before serving add a block of ice.

Champagne Fruit Punch

- 1 bottle inexpensive champagne
- 3 quarts raspberry soda
- 1/2 gallon inexpensive raspberry sherbet

Thoroughly chill soda, champagne, and punch bowl. Spoon all the sherbet into the punch bowl. Pour raspberry soda and champagne over the top of the sherbet, which will create a foamy, pink punch.

Comforting Christmas Nog

- 12 egg yolks
- 1 pound powdered sugar
- 1 quart dark rum or brandy
- 2-1/2 quarts whipping cream
- 1 quart whole milk
- 6 egg whites
- 1/2 teaspoon salt
- Freshly grated nutmeg

Beat egg yolks until light in color. Beat in powdered sugar, liquor, cream and milk. Cover and refrigerate for at least 4 hours. Beat egg whites until stiff and fold lightly with the salt and combine with the chilled mixture. Top each serving with freshly grated nutmeg.

Wonderful Wassail

- 5 medium baking apples
- 1 cup sugar
- 1/4 cup water
- 3 cups ale
- 3-1/2 cups apple cider
- 1 teaspoon allspice

Core apples and sprinkle with 1/2 cup sugar. Add water and bake at 375 degrees for 30 minutes, or until tender. Combine ale, cider, remaining sugar, and allspice in saucepan and place over low heat. Stir until sugar is dissolved, but do not boil. Place roasted apples in punch bowl and pour ale mixture over them.

Mimosa Punch

- 2 bottles inexpensive chilled champagne
- 2 quarts chilled orange juice
- 12 sliced strawberries
- Frozen orange juice cubes
- Fresh mint garnish

Combine all ingredients except mint garnish in six-quart punch bowl. As punch is served, garnish each cup with a sprig of mint.

Small-Budget Children's Party Recipes

I have divided the children's party recipes into these categories:

- Snacks.
- Salads.
- Mini-meals.
- Desserts.

Snacks

Popcorn Balls

Roll six cups of popped corn in eight ounces of melted vanilla caramel candies mixed with one tablespoon butter (microwave for one minute on high to melt the caramel.) Shape the coated popcorn into small balls. Wrap each in plastic wrap and tie with a bow.

Popcorn Roasted over the Fire

Let the children pop their own popcorn over the fire using a campfire popcorn popper.

Painted Toast

The children paint pieces of bread using food coloring and paint brushes; then toast.

Celery Stuffed with Peanut Butter

Wash celery stalks and pat dry; fill with peanut butter. Cut into 3-inch pieces and serve.

Bowls of Sugared Cereal

Children love to snack on sugared cereal served dry in bowls.

Other snacks

- One Box of Animal Crackers per Child.
- Fortune Cookies.

Salads

Poison Spider Salad

Spread each plate with large lettuce leaves. Place a large canned pear half upside down on top of the lettuce. Press red hots into the tops of the pear halves. Add licorice or black pipe cleaner legs.

Pineapple Boat Kebobs

Hollow out half of a fresh pineapple cut lengthwise; fill with pineapple chunks, maraschino cherries, grapes, banana slices, and cheese and ham chunks, all skewered with ruffled toothpicks.

Watermelon Boat

Cut a watermelon in half. Scoop the watermelon out in balls, using a melon baller. Place the watermelon balls back into the shell, along with mini-scoops of raspberry sherbet.

Jell-O Jiggles

Prepare Jell-O, decreasing the amount of water by 25 percent. For example, if the recipe calls for one cup boiling water and one cup cold water, decrease the cold water to 1/2 cup. Pour Jell-O into a shallow pan. When gelled, cut into squares or shapes, using a knife or cookie cutters. Or, pour Jell-O into small paper cups, drop one gummy bear into each one and set in the refrigerator. When ready to serve, place the cups in lukewarm water for a few seconds, then unmold onto a serving plate.

Make-Your-Own Fruit Kabobs

Provide one wooden skewer per child, along with bowls of bite-sized fresh fruits, such as pineapple chunks, grapes, melon balls, orange sections, strawberries and cherries. Decorate the end of each skewer with crinkle ribbon. Let each child create his own kabob by sliding pieces of fruit onto his skewer, then eating one piece at a time.

Mini-Meals

Hot Dogs and Beans

Let the children roast their own hot dogs over a campfire or the flames in your fireplace. Tuck them into buns, add mustard, and serve alongside a mound of baked beans and corn-on-the-cob. For something different, here's a cowpoke favorite: Cut the hot dogs into small, bite-sized pieces, dip them in pancake batter, and deep fry in a skillet or wok.

Bean Boats

Split hamburger buns and place them with flat surface up on cookie sheets. Butter the buns and top with layers of canned pork and beans, grated cheddar cheese, and imitation bacon bits. Place under broiler until bubbling and browned.

Waffle Surprise

Toast two frozen waffles. Spread one with pineapple cream cheese and raspberry jam, the other with chunky peanut butter and chopped peanuts. Put the two halves together and serve.

Do-It-Yourself Shish Kabobs

Provide the children with blunt-tipped wooden skewers, plus bowls of bite-sized pineapple, brown-and-serve sausage links, sour dough French bread, baked ham, bananas, apples, and tomatoes. Let the children skewer their own kabobs, cover with butter-flavored cooking spray, and cook over a barbecue or campfire. The meats have been pre-cooked so there is no fear of undercooked foods.

Peanut Butter Banana Dogs

Fill a foot-long hot dog bun with sliced bananas, gobs of peanut butter, chopped nuts, and M & M candies.

Miniature Hamburgers and Potato Chips or French Fries

Serve miniature hamburgers (use baking powder biscuits for buns).

Personal Potato Toppers

Provide one baked potato per child, along with toppings: hot chili; sour cream; imitation bacon bits; cooked hamburger with taco seasoning; grated cheeses; crumbled tortilla chips; and sliced black olives. Let each child create his own potato meal.

Hero Sandwiches

Slice a whole loaf of French bread in half lengthwise. Let the children help you fill the bottom layer with mustard; relish; pickle slices; pepperoni; lunchmeats; sliced cheeses; sliced tomatoes; lettuce; and so forth. Then, place the "lid" on the sandwich and cut into child-sized portions.

Giant Pancake with Fruit Topping

Cook giant pancakes in a round cast-iron skillet. Serve in the skillet, topped with fresh berries and piles of whipped cream.

Animal Sandwiches

Cut sandwiches into animal shapes, using a cookie cutter.

Macaroni and Cheese

Boxed or homemade, kids love this stuff!

Personalized Pizzas

Prepare individual eight-inch pizzas using refrigerated pizza dough, canned pizza sauce, and shredded mozzarella and cheddar cheeses. Make "faces" with cherry tomato noses, sliced green pepper lips, and black olive eyes. Bake according to the directions on the pizza dough package.

Muffin Pizzas

Provide the children with English muffins, along with grated cheeses; pizza sauce; black olive slices; pepperoni pieces; and so forth. Let the children design their own custom mini-pizzas.

Pizza Cups

- 1 pkg. Pillsbury ready-made pizza dough
- 1 jar pizza sauce
- 1 pkg. shredded cheddar and mozzarella cheese
- Fillings (chopped olives, pepperoni pieces, bacon bits, canned mushrooms, canned pineapple chunks, or other toppings.)

The guests make their own individual pizza cups by patting pizza dough into muffin tins, then adding fillings. Place muffin tin on cookie sheet and bake at 375 degrees for approximately 15 minutes. Watch carefully so it doesn't overcook.

Do-It-Yourself Taco Bar

Lay out large heated taco shells and all the ingredients: cooked ground beef; chopped tomatoes; shredded lettuce; diced green chilies; chopped olives; shredded cheeses; salsa and sour cream.

Pigs-in-a-Blanket

Wrap biscuit dough around canned cocktail weiners and bake them in the oven until the dough has browned on top.

Smashed Sandwich Rolls

Use a rolling pin to flatten pieces of white bread. Cover each piece with peanut butter, jelly, and a few mini-marshmallows. Roll up tight and cut into bite-sized slices.

Mega-Hamburger

Roll two pounds of hamburger meat into a flat hamburger the size of a dinner plate and cook well. Serve between two halves of a round loaf of Hawaiian bread, cut in half horizontally. Top the burger with the usual tomato, lettuce and condiments. Slice into pie-shaped pieces and serve.

Corn Dogs Dipped in Mustard

Step 1: Get a corndog.
Step 2: Dip it in mustard.
Step 3: Eat; repeat Steps 1 and 2.

Desserts

S'Mores

Let the children roast large marshmallows over a fire, using sticks or straightened coat hangers. As soon as they begin to brown, help the children smash the marshmallows and half a flat chocolate bar between two graham crackers.

Sherbet Parfaits

Fill tall clear glasses with alternating scoops of sherbet and Cool Whip. Top with Cool Whip, candy sprinkles, and a cherry.

Snowballs

Roll scoops of firm vanilla ice cream in flaky coconut.

Marshmallow Fondue Dip

This is *really* messy, so you might want to take this project to the patio! Provide fondue forks, large marshmallows, and a fondue pot full of warm chocolate sauce. Let the children skewer the marshmallows, dip them into the chocolate and eat them.

Frozen Fruit Balls

Cut the top off a large orange. Scoop out the fruit and its juice. Decorate the oranges with happy faces, using black felt-tip permanent markers. Fill the empty orange shells with scoops of orange sherbet and freeze until ready to serve.

Edible Headbands

Sew wrapped candies together using long strands of dental floss cut into headband lengths, with three or four inches left over for tying. Tie a piece of curled crinkle ribbon at each juncture of candy, hiding the dental floss and decorating the headband. The children may want to make their own headbands. They make excellent party favors.

Rocky Road Sandwiches

Slice chocolate cupcakes in half to make a "top" and "bottom" for each sandwich. Place a *small* scoop of rocky road ice cream between the halves, press together, and serve. **Option:** In place of cupcake halves, use large flat cookies.

Candy Cones

Fill flat-bottomed ice cream cones with small candies; tie ribbon around the top of each cone.

Snow Cones

Fill paper cups with real snow or crushed ice from the blender with red fruit juice.

Tasty Party Necklaces

Provide long, thin strands of licorice and bowls of donut-shaped dry cereals, such as Cheerios and Trix. Let the children make their own party necklaces by threading the licorice through the cereal pieces and tying the ends together with a double knot.

Decorate-Your-Own Cupcakes

Place a plastic tablecloth over your table. Set out cupcakes; frostings; frosting tubes; candy sprinkles; and novelty cake decorations. Provide the children with plastic knives; let them decorate their own cupcakes. Furnish pipe cleaners and red licorice strips to be used as "handles." Press the ends of the pipe cleaners or licorice into the sides of the cupcakes to convert them into "baskets."

Cupcake Carousels

After cupcakes have baked and cooled, carefully remove the cupcake papers. Frost top and sides of each cupcake. Place a miniature paper umbrella in the center of each cupcake. "Hold up" the umbrella with small candy canes, straight pretzels, or colored plastic toothpicks. Press animal crackers into the sides of the cupcakes.

Sugar Cookies

- 1 cup melted butter
- 1 1/2 cups sifted confectioners' sugar
- 1 egg
- 1 1/2 teaspoon vanilla
- 2 1/2 cups all-purpose flour, sifted

- 1 teaspoon baking soda
- 1 teaspoon cream of tartar
- Canned white frosting
- Food colorings

Mix the first four ingredients together thoroughly. Sift the flour, baking soda, and cream of tartar together and add this mixture to the first four ingredients. Cover and chill for three hours. Heat oven to 375 degrees. Roll the dough on a lightly floured cloth-covered board until it is approximately 1/4 inch thick. Cut into desired shapes and bake on lightly greased baking sheet for 7 or 8 minutes until lightly brown on the edges. Let cool and frost.

Dirt Pie

- One small clay flower pot per guest (or one sturdy plastic cup)
- One large plastic drinking straw per guest
- Rocky road ice cream
- Oreo cookies
- Single-stemmed fresh flowers, preferably daisies, tulips, or daffodils

Wash flower pots well and let them dry thoroughly. Place one Oreo cookie over the hole at the bottom of each clay pot. Fill each pot with rocky road ice cream to within one inch from the top. Insert a straw in the center of the ice cream and cover the rest with crushed Oreo cookies. Freeze until time to serve. Insert the stem of one fresh flower into each straw before serving.

Gummy Worm Cake

Bake any kind of cake or cupcakes. Press gummy worms down inside the cake after it has baked. Frost the cake and add more gummy worms on top.

Cupcake Spiders

Remove the cupcake paper from a chocolate cupcake. Frost the top and sides of the cupcake with thick white icing. Add eight black licorice "legs" (four on each side), chocolate sprinkles, and red hot candies for the eyes.

Cupcake Birthday Cake

Instead of a standard birthday cake, bake cupcakes and decorate each with a letter that spells out "Happy Birthday [NAME] ".

Tip: Use Lifesaver candies, marshmallows, or gumdrops as novelty candleholders on the cake.

Small-Budget Adult Party Recipes

have divided the adult fare into these categories:

- Snacks and appetizers.
- Luncheon buffet.
- Informal supper dishes.
- Formal dinner menu.
- Party desserts.

Snacks and Appetizers

Fruit and Cheese Tray

Arrange fresh fruits and cheeses on a tray. Strawberries, melons, and grapes are popular choices because they hold up well and have a showy appearance.

Mexican Nachos

Combine shredded jack cheese and shredded cheddar cheese (three parts jack to one part cheddar) and microwave on high for two minutes, stirring half way through. Serve with large tortilla chips.

Parmesan Mushrooms

- 3 pounds large fresh mushrooms
- 6 tablespoons extra virgin olive oil
- 3/4 cup finely chopped green onions
- 2 cups finely chopped red bell pepper

- 1/2 cup no-fat mayonnaise
- 1/4 cup Dijon mustard
- 1 teaspoon garlic power
- 1 teaspoon dried oregano
- 1 tablespoon red wine
- 4 tablespoons grated Parmesan cheese

Remove mushroom stems. Roll mushrooms in oil and broil (caps right side up) for 6 to 8 minutes until tender. Chop the mushroom stems and add to the onions and bell pepper; sauté in oil for 4 minutes; add wine and sauté for another minute. Add the mayo and mustard. Stir mixture well and spoon one teaspoonful into each mushroom cap. Sprinkle with the Parmesan cheese and broil until brown. (12 servings)

Party Gorp

Mix these ingredients together and serve in bowls or baskets:

Peanuts	Sunflower seeds
Raisins	Chocolate chips
M&Ms	Chopped dates

Snack Mix

- 1 box Wheat Chex
- 1 box Rice Chex
- 1 box Corn Chex
- 1 large can mixed nuts
- 1 large jar peanuts
- 1 package thin pretzels
- 1 pound butter
- 2 tablespoons chili powder
- 1 tablespoon onion salt
- 1/4 cup Worcestershire sauce

Pour the cereals, nuts, and pretzels into a flat metal baking pan. Melt butter and seasonings together over a low heat. Pour over the cereal/nut mixture and bake in 250 degree oven for 45 minutes.

Chip 'N Dips

Along with any kind of sturdy chips, serve one or more of these homemade dips:

Horseradish Crab Dip
- 2-1/2 cups imitation crab meat, shredded
- 3 8-ounce packages light Neufchatel cream cheese, softened
- 1-1/2 cups undiluted evaporated skimmed milk
- 1/2 cup finely sliced green onions
- 1/2 cup finely chopped red bell pepper
- 1 teaspoon garlic salt
- 2 teaspoons prepared horseradish

Whip the milk and cream cheese together; stir in the rest of the ingredients. Cover and refrigerate for two hours. (Makes 6 cups)

Creamy Spinach Dip in a Bread Bowl
- 3 large round sourdough loaves of French bread
- 4 cups low-fat yogurt
- 2 10-ounce packages of frozen chopped spinach, thawed and squeezed dry
- 1/2 cup mayonnaise
- 2 packages dry onion soup mix

Mix together the yogurt, spinach, mayonnaise, and onion soup mix, cover and chill in the refrigerator for up to 4 hours. Use a sharp knife to hollow out the loaves of French bread. Fill the bread "bowls" with the spinach mixture and serve with the scooped-out bread pieces, which can be used as "dippers." (20 servings)

Cilantro Bean Dip
- 2 15-oz. cans drained black beans
- 1 cup non-fat mayonnaise
- 1 cup low fat sour cream
- 2 4-oz. cans chopped green chilies, drained
- 1/4 cup chopped cilantro
- 2 teaspoons chili powder
- 1 teaspoon garlic powder
- 2 teaspoons hot sauce

Mash beans with a fork or use slow speed in food processor. Mix in remaining ingredients, cover, and refrigerate for one hour. (Makes 5 cups)

Strawberry Ring

Arrange large fresh strawberries in a ring around a bowl of confectioners sugar for dipping.

Broiled Cocktail Sausages

Cut a cabbage into two halves and place cut-side down on two plates. Broil cocktail sausages. Skewer them with long wooden or plastic party picks and stick them into the cabbages, capping each pick with a black olive.

Tortilla Wrap

- 15 flour tortillas
- 1-1/2 cups refried beans
- 1 cup shredded cheddar cheese
- 6 chopped green onions
- 1/2 cup chopped black olives

Mix ingredients together. Spread on tortillas. Roll tortillas as tightly as possible and bake at 375 degrees for 10 minutes.

Luncheon buffet

Peach Coleslaw

- 4 cups shredded cabbage
- 1/2 cup chopped bell pepper
- 1 large can sliced peaches, drained
- 1 cup chopped celery
- 1-1/2 cups miniature marshmallows
- Enough mayonnaise to moisten

Combine ingredients, mix well, and chill. (10 servings)

Creamy Waldorf Salad

- 4 cups diced red delicious apples
- 2 tablespoons sugar
- 2 cups diced celery
- 1 teaspoon lemon juice
- 2 cups walnut pieces
- Dash of salt
- 1/2 cup mayonnaise
- 1 cup whipped cream

Mix together the mayonnaise, sugar, lemon juice, salt, and whipped cream. Add apples, celery, and walnuts, then chill. (12 servings)

Tomato Flower Potato Salad

- 12 extra-large chilled tomatoes
- 2 teaspoons salt
- 12 medium potatoes
- 1/2 teaspoon pepper
- 1/2 cup finely chopped red onion
- 1/2 cup Italian salad dressing
- 1 cup chopped celery
- 1 cup mayonnaise
- 4 hard-boiled eggs, cut up
- 2 tablespoons mustard
- 1 head red leaf lettuce
- 1 small can sliced ripe olives

Boil potatoes in salted water until tender. Drain, cool, and peel. Cut potatoes into small cubes. Combine with onion, celery, and eggs. Combine salad dressing, mayonnaise, mustard, salt, and pepper and add to potato mixture. Cover and refrigerate for 3 to 4 hours. Cut off stem ends of chilled tomatoes, to give them flat bottoms for stability. With cut side down, cut each tomato into sixths, cutting through within 1/2 inch of the bottom. *Carefully* spread the sections apart, forming a "flower." Fill tomatoes with chilled potato mixture, top with olives and serve on large platter lined with red leaf lettuce.

Tossed Green Salad

Tear your favorite lettuce into bite-sized pieces and combine with sliced tomatoes, green onions, artichoke hearts, fresh sliced mushrooms, canned garbanzo beans, and slices of avocado. Serve with a variety of dressings on the side.

Pineapple Boats

Cut a fresh pineapple in half lengthways. Scoop out the pineapple and cut into small pieces. Mix the pineapple with grapes, cherries, melon pieces, nuts and coconut. Add two wooden skewers to the sides of the "boat" as oars. Make a "sail" by attaching a triangle of heavy white paper to the top of a wooden skewer, which is embedded into the salad.

Taco Salad

- 2 pounds ground beef
- 2 pounds canned red kidney beans

- 1/2 teaspoon salt
- 1/2 teaspoon pepper
- 1/2 teaspoon garlic powder
- 1 head lettuce, torn into small pieces
- 2 large tomatoes, cubed
- 1 cup grated cheddar cheese
- 4 scallions, sliced
- 2 cups crushed tortilla chips
- 2 cups salsa

Brown beef and drain well. Add drained beans and seasonings and cook at low heat for 5 minutes. Toss together with the lettuce, tomato, avocado, scallions, cheese and tortilla chips. Top with salsa and serve. (Serves 12 to 14)

Tijuana Tamale Pie

- 1 1/2 pounds ground beef
- 2 small cans sliced black olives
- 5 cups milk
- 2 1/4 cups yellow cornmeal
- 4 beaten eggs
- 1 pound grated Cheddar cheese
- 2 cans (7 oz.) whole kernel corn
- 2 teaspoons garlic salt
- 2 teaspoons chili powder
- 1 large jar medium hot salsa
- 2 cans (14 1/2 oz) whole peeled tomatoes, undrained and cut up
- 2 packages Lawry's Spices & Seasonings for Chili (or Lawry's Taco Spices & Seasonings)

Brown ground beef until crumbly and drain well. In a large bowl combine milk, 2 cups cornmeal, and eggs. Add beef and remaining ingredients, except for the cheese and 1/4 cup of cornmeal. Stir together and pour into two lightly greased 12 x 8 x 2-inch baking dishes. Bake uncovered in 350 degree oven for 40 to 45 minutes. Sprinkle with the cheese and remaining cornmeal; continue baking until cheese melts and cornmeal is browned. Let stand for 10 minutes before serving. Serve with salsa. (Serves 16)

Reuben Sandwiches

- Black rye bread
- Swiss cheese
- Corned beef, cooked & sliced
- Canned sauerkraut
- Butter
- Thousand island dressing
- Hot mustard

For each sandwich, butter all sides of two pieces of bread. On inside of sandwich, spread hot mustard on one piece of bread and the dressing on the other. Drain sauerkraut *well*. Place a layer of corned beef, a layer of sauerkraut, and a layer of Swiss cheese. Grill sandwich on medium heat until cheese is melted.

Informal supper dishes

Informal suppers lend themselves to potluck, with each guest bringing a different course. You, as host, can fill in with the main dish or the dessert. This is a great way to cut costs, and everyone still has a good time. Here are some economical favorites:

Swedish Meatballs

- 2 pounds ground chuck
- 1/2 cup butter
- 1 pound ground pork
- 2 yellow onions, minced
- 2 eggs, slightly beaten
- 1/2 teaspoon nutmeg
- 2 tablespoons cornstarch
- 1/2 teaspoon ground ginger
- 1 cup hot milk
- 3 teaspoons salt
- 2 tablespoons flour
- 1/4 teaspoon allspice
- 1 teaspoon pepper

Mix meat, eggs, milk, and cornstarch together. Add all the rest of the ingredients, except for the flour and butter. Form mixture into small balls and brown in the butter. Add a little water and simmer slowly for about 40 minutes. Remove the meatballs from the pan and make a gravy out of the drippings by adding the flour and enough water for a medium thick gravy. (20 servings)

Potato Casserole

- 4 pounds cooked, mashed potatoes
- 2 teaspoons salt
- 2 pounds canned Danish bacon
- 1/2 teaspoon white pepper
- 6 medium yellow onions
- 4 cups cubed pickled beets
- Chopped parsley

Dice bacon and onions and sauté in butter until onions are tender. Add seasonings to the mashed potatoes. Place potatoes in large casserole dish and pour the drained bacon and onions over the top. Bake in 300 degree oven for 10 minutes. Garnish with pickled beets and parsley. (20 servings)

Fried Bratwurst

Purchase 1 bratwurst per guest. Fry the bratwurst in butter, turning frequently until golden brown on all sides. Cover the bratwurst with water and simmer uncovered for 20 minutes. Serve with hot mustard or sour cream.

Italian Pasta Bar

Let your guests customize their own pasta dishes.
- Hot spaghetti and fettuccini noodles
- Your own homemade spaghetti sauce, or
- A variety of ready-made specialty sauces by Five Brothers, Prego or Classico, such as:
  - Tomato and Basil
  - Italian Sausage and Fennel
  - Mushrooms and Ripe Olives
  - Roasted Peppers and Onions
  - Sun-dried Tomato
  - Creamy Mushroom
  - Alfredo with Mushrooms
  - Tomato Alfredo
  - Garlic and Herb

- Tomato, Spinach and Cheese
- Vegetable Primavera
- Florentine Spinach and Cheese

Grilled Corn on the Cob

Soak the corn (husk and all) under water for about 15 minutes. Then lay the corn, still in its husks, over hot barbecue coals for about 20 minutes, turning *constantly*.

Grilled Red Potatoes

Split potatoes, sprinkle with garlic salt and spray with buttered-flavored oil. Wrap in heavy-duty foil and place over hottest barbecue coals for about 30 minutes.

Hamburger Pie

Trust me: Men love this!

- 2 pounds ground round
- 2 cans condensed tomato soup
- 2 onions, chopped
- 10 boiled potatoes, mashed
- 1 teaspoon salt
- 1 cup warm milk
- 1/2 teaspoon pepper
- 2 cans cut green beans, drained
- 2 eggs, beaten
- 1 cup grated cheddar cheese
- Two baked pie shells

In a large skillet cook meat and onion until meat is brown and onion is tender. Add salt and pepper. Add drained beans and soup. Pour mixture into the pie shells. Mash potatoes while they are still hot; add milk and eggs. Spoon mounds of mashed potatoes over the meat mixture. Sprinkle potatoes with the grated cheese. Bake at 350 degrees for about 25 minutes. (8 servings)

Formal dinner menu

Note: This is the affordable formal dinner menu suggested in Chapter 40 (Cruise Ship Formal Night Dinner Party), but it may be used for any formal dinner party.

- Parmesan Mushroom Appetizer
- Vichyssoise (potato soup)
- Baby Spinach Mandarin Salad
- Coq au vin (Chicken in wine)
- Cheese Stuffed Tomatoes
- Asparagus Tips with Hollandaise Sauce
- Baguettes with Garlic
- Dessert Cheeses
- Baked Alaska
- After-dinner mints

And now, the recipes (**Note:** These recipes serve eight.):

Parmesan Mushroom Appetizers

(see recipe on page 181 in "Snacks & Appetizers")

Vichyssoise

This elegant French soup is actually quite easy to prepare if you use instant potatoes (no one will ever know!) And, of course, it can be cooked ahead of time and left in your refrigerator until served.

- 2 small yellow onions, grated
- 2 tablespoons instant chicken bouillon
- 2 cups water
- 1/2 teaspoon salt
- 4 cups whole milk
- 2 1/2 cups instant dry mashed potatoes
- 2 cups cream
- Chopped chives

Combine onion, bouillon, water and salt in large kettle. Heat to boiling. Reduce heat, cover and simmer for 15 minutes. Remove from heat. Add milk and instant potatoes. Whip until fluffy. Gradually stir in remaining milk and heat *just* to boiling point. Cover and chill in refrigerator. Just before serving, stir in the cold cream, beating vigorously with a fork until blended. Serve topped with chopped chives.

Baby Spinach Mandarin Salad

- 2 bunches fresh baby spinach
- 1 large can (15 oz.) mandarin oranges
- Raspberry vinaigrette

- 1/2 cup raspberry vinegar
- 1/2 cup virgin olive oil
- 1/2 teaspoon pepper
- 1/4 teaspoon salt
- 1 tablespoon sugar
- 2 tablespoons chopped chives

Remove stems and any browned pieces from spinach. Tear spinach into bite-sized pieces, wash and chill. Combine all ingredients in large plastic bag, shake well and serve with chilled salad forks on chilled salad plates.

Coq au Vin

- 8 large chicken breasts, split*
- 1 teaspoon salt
- 8 pieces of bacon, diced
- 1/2 teaspoon pepper
- 2 cups chopped scallions
- 2 cups red wine
- 1 pound mushroom pieces
- 2 cups chicken broth
- 1 tablespoon crushed fresh garlic

Sauté bacon and onions in a skillet until nicely browned. Add chicken breasts and brown well. Place bacon, onion, chicken breasts, and remaining ingredients in large slow cooker, such as a Crock-Pot. Cover and cook on low for 8 hours. (* Allow one chicken breast per guest.)

Asparagus Tips with Hollandaise Sauce

- 3 pounds frozen asparagus tips
- Two bottles Hollandaise sauce

This elegant dish is so easy it's embarrassing! Cook asparagus according to directions on the package. Pour the Hollandaise into your prettiest gravy server and dribble over asparagus as it is served onto guests' plates.

Cheese Stuffed Tomatoes

- 8 large tomatoes
- 1/2 cup chopped scallions
- 1 cup grated cheddar cheese

Cut off tops of tomatoes and gently hollow out the centers. Save the pulp. Combine the pulp and cheese in a blender; blend until smooth. Stir in chopped onions and spoon into hollowed tomatoes. Place tomatoes in muffin tin and bake at 350 degrees for 12 to 15 minutes. Remove tomatoes very carefully with a large spoon.

Baguettes with Garlic

- 3 baguette French bread loaves, sliced thin
- Olive oil
- Garlic powder

Drizzle olive oil over bread slices and sprinkle with garlic powder. Place slices face up on cookie sheet and bake at 350 degrees for approximately 10 minutes; watch carefully so they don't get too browned.

Baked Alaska

See recipe under "Party Desserts", except that this Baked Alaska receives special treatment by adding lighted sparklers or tall tapered candles.

Dessert Cheeses

Once the dessert has been served, bring out a tray of dessert cheeses, such as French Brie, American Liederkranz, American Camembert, Gouda, Edam, and Gruyere.

Party Desserts

Blueberry Surprise

It's hard to believe that a serving of anything this delicious only has 135 calories and 2 grams of fat, but it's true!

- 1/2 gallon non-fat vanilla ice cream or frozen yogurt
- 3 small cantaloupes, thinly sliced and peeled
- 3 cups fresh or frozen blueberries (or you can use raspberries or strawberries)
- 2 1/2 cups orange juice
- 2 1/4 tablespoons cornstarch
- 2/3 cup sugar

In a small saucepan stir together the sugar and cornstarch. Add the orange juice and berries. Cook and stir until beginning to thicken, then cook for two more minutes. Cool in refrigerator for 20 minutes. Scoop 1/3 cup ice cream or yogurt into each dessert dish. Arrange cantaloupe slices on one side of the dish. Pour berry sauce over top of ice cream or yogurt. Serve immediately. (20 servings)

Do-It-Yourself Sundaes

Serve bowls filled with scoops of various flavors of ice cream. Then let the guests make their own sundaes by adding: sauces, such as chocolate, hot fudge, butterscotch, or caramel; fruits, including strawberries, raspberries, boysenberries, sliced bananas or peaches; chopped walnuts, almonds, pecans, or peanuts; and whipped topping, such as Cool Whip or fresh-whipped whipping cream.

Swedish Macaroon Tea Cakes

- 4 cups sifted flour
- 1 cup sugar
- 2 cups softened butter
- 2 eggs
- 1 tablespoon vanilla

Cream sugar and butter together and then beat in the eggs and vanilla. Stir in the flour and mix well. Drop a rounded teaspoonful of batter into each greased tiny muffin cup, pressing batter over the bottom and up around the sides, a coating about 1/4 inch thick. Chill and then fill each hollow with:

Almond Macaroon Filling

- 4 eggs
- 1 cup sugar
- 1 teaspoon almond extract
- 3 cups finely chopped almonds

Beat eggs until foamy. Add sugar and mix until blended. Add almonds and almond extract. Bake at 325 degrees for about 25 minutes, until browned and set. (Makes 4 dozen tea cakes)

Raspberry Lemon Trifle

Now, here's a nice surprise: something that looks *spectacular*, but takes very little work!

- Two large boxes of ladyfingers
- Brandy or fruit liqueur
- One large package of frozen raspberries
- One jar of apricot preserves
- One large package of lemon pudding mix
- Whipping cream
- A clear glass bowl with high sides

Alternate layers of ladyfingers, drizzled with the brandy or liqueur and layers of the preserves, thawed raspberries, and prepared pudding. Top with a layer of fruit piled with freshly whipped cream. Refrigerate for at least one hour. (20 servings)

 **A tip.** For a dramatic flare, turn the lights down low and enter the room carrying any of these desserts topped with lighted sparklers!

Irish Appleberry Crunch

- 1 1/2 pounds apples
- 1 1/2 pounds blackberries
- 1/4 cup water
- 1 1/2 cups sugar
- 2 sticks butter
- 2 cups flour
- 1-1/3 cup oatmeal
- 1/2 cup dark brown sugar

Peel, core, and slice the apples. Add to washed blackberries and place in a large shallow baking pan. Dribble the water and sugar over the top.

Combine softened butter, flour, oatmeal, and brown sugar in a bowl and mix together until all the ingredients stick together and become crumbly. Spread these crumbly pieces over the top of the fruit, packing down lightly. Bake in preheated 400 degree oven for 15 minutes. Then reduce heat to 375 degrees and cook for another 15 to 20 minutes, or until cooked through and crunchy on top. Serve warm with whipped cream or vanilla ice cream. (Serves 16)

Baked Alaska

- 1 quart brick-shaped ice cream of your choice
- 4 egg whites
- 1/2 cup superfine sugar

1. Remove ice cream from carton, place on oven-proof serving plate and put in the freezer uncovered for 30 minutes.
2. Pre-heat oven to 450 degrees.
3. Beat 4 egg whites until stiff; continue beating as you add the sugar a little at a time. Take the ice cream out of the freezer and cover entirely with the meringue as quickly as you can (or the ice cream will start to melt.) Bake in 450 degree oven for 5 minutes or until the peaks of meringue are beginning to brown. Serve immediately (or as soon as possible after "marching around the room"; see Chapter 40).

Cappuccino Cookie Float

Pour 3 or 4 tablespoons of chocolate syrup in the bottom of a tall clear glass. Add one crumbled cookie* and one scoop chocolate ice cream. Pour iced cappuccino** over the ice cream, to within an inch of the top of the glass. Add a small scoop of praline ice cream, a squirt of whipped cream and another cookie which should be stuck into the side of the praline ice cream.

> * Pepperidge Farm Chocolate Laced Pirouettes Cookies (delicate "rolled" cookies that look like tiny stovepipes)
> ** Use any instant cappuccino mix, such as General Foods International Coffees, Maxwell House, or Nescafe

Melon Ball Compotes

- 1/2 gallon raspberry sherbet
- 10 cups melon balls
- 3 cups chilled ginger ale

For each serving, surround one scoop of sherbet with six or eight small melon balls. Pour 1/4 cup ginger ale over the top. (12 servings)

Part

6

Small-Budget Party Worksheets

The worksheets that follow have been created to help you:

- Know what to do and when to do it.
- Stay organized.
- Establish your party budget.

These worksheets won't do you a bit of good, however, unless you use them. The biggest mistake you can make is to try to keep track of everything in your head. Take it from me: If you want the planning to be easy and successful, don't trust your memory. Although a brain isn't a computer, it *is* known to become overloaded and drop data from time to time, especially when it's under stress. So get in the habit of using these worksheets as you plan any of your parties.

By the way, feel free to take these worksheets to a copy center where they can be enlarged to fit a three-ring notebook, a handy tool to keep you on track and make your party the easiest and most successful one you've ever hosted.

To-do Lists

ere are lists that will help you with your planning. Use the right hand column to record the date each task has been completed.

Things that can be done weeks in advance

Date Done

☐ Enlist a co-host and/or volunteers to help with the party. _____

☐ Confer with your guest(s) of honor, if applicable, regarding a convenient date and time for the party. _____

☐ Choose a location for the party. _____

☐ Choose a party theme. _____

☐ Hand-craft or purchase invitations. _____

☐ Assemble a guest list with addresses. _____

☐ Address and mail invitations. _____

☐ Plan a menu, including detailed recipes, a shopping list, and a list of foods that can be prepared or purchased in advance and placed in the freezer. _____

Date Done

☐ Plan the entertainment, including games, activities, door prizes, music and toasts.

_____

☐ Make or purchase favors.

_____

☐ Purchase prizes.

_____

☐ Make or purchase name tags.

_____

☐ Make or purchase place cards.

_____

☐ Make, purchase, borrow, or rent decorations.

_____

☐ Purchase film or single-use cameras.

_____

☐ Assemble and clean all crystal, china, silver,
linens, etc.

_____

☐ Decide what you're going to wear to the party
and get it ready, including hose, shoes, and
accessories.

_____

Other:

☐ _____   _____

☐ _____   _____

☐ _____   _____

☐ _____   _____

☐ _____   _____

☐ _____   _____

☐ _____   _____

☐ _____   _____

☐ _____   _____

Things that can be done one week before the party

Date Done

☐ Call any guests who have not responded to your RSVP to see if they are coming. _____

☐ Once you know how many guests are coming, start filling out the name tags and place cards. _____

To be done 1 or 2 days before the party

☐ Shop for perishable food items and prepare them as far as you can ahead of time (dicing; marinating; rinsing lettuce, etc.). _____

☐ Pick up any rented or borrowed decorations and start decorating your site. _____

☐ Call to confirm arrangements with musicians, entertainers, etc. _____

☐ Call your guest(s) of honor and anyone who has volunteered to help you with the party to confirm their time of arrival. _____

☐ If the guests will be wearing coats or jackets, clear out your coat closet and fill it with quality hangers. _____

To be done the day of the party

☐ Last-minute cooking and baking. _____

☐ Last-minute decorating, including fresh flowers for the guest bathroom and any exterior decorating (balloons tied to gate, etc.). _____

☐ If you will be serving a sit-down meal, arrange the place cards in a creative way, whereby each guest is seated next to someone he doesn't know. (Be sure to separate spouses.) _____

☐ If you will be serving food from a buffet table, scatter TV trays around the room or provide lap trays for the guests.

☐ If you plan to serve snacks or appetizers, set them out *before* your guests are scheduled to arrive.

Date Done

_____

_____

Other:

☐ _____   _____

☐ _____   _____

☐ _____   _____

☐ _____   _____

☐ _____   _____

☐ _____   _____

☐ _____   _____

☐ _____   _____

☐ _____   _____

Small-Budget Party Planner

Master Budget

Category	Amount Budgeted	Final Cost
Party Site	$	$
Party Decorations	$	$
Game Supplies	$	$
Door Prizes	$	$
Party Menu	$	$
Entertainment	$	$
Party Rentals	$	$
Other:	$	$
Other:	$	$
Other:	$	$
	Total final cost of the party:	$

Conclusion

I hope you've found some creative, afford-able party ideas in this book. I sure had fun putting them together for you. In fact, as I gathered information for this book I real-ized even more than ever before how easy it is to entertain on a small budget. It isn't how much you *spend* on your party; it's how much *love* you put into it. The key isn't to spend gobs of money, but to show how much you care by the time and effort you put into the planning, and by being creative as you personalize the party for the occasion. A party planned from a loving heart will be a successful party every time.

I'll be updating this book from time to time, and I'd love to hear about your small-budget party ideas. Please drop me a note through my publisher:

Diane Warner
c/o Career Press/New Page Books
P.O. Box 687
Franklin Lakes, NJ 07417

Meanwhile, please drop by and visit me anytime at my Web site: *www.dianewarnerbooks.com*

Index

About the Author

Diane Warner has authored 20 books and is nationally respected as America's favorite authority on weddings and parties. Her best-selling books include *Complete Book of Wedding Vows*; *Complete Book of Wedding Toasts*; *Complete Book of Wedding Showers*; *Complete Book of Baby Showers*; *Diane Warner's Complete Book of Children's Parties*; *Diane Warner's Big Book of Parties*; and *How to Have a Big Wedding on a Small Budget, 3rd Edition*. She also writes for newspapers, magazines, and Web sites; conducts seminars; and appears regularly on national television, including HGTV, Discovery Channel, and CNN. She has two grown children and lives with her author-husband in Tucson, Arizona.

Also by Diane Warner:

- *Diane Warner's Big Book of Parties*
- *Diane Warner's Complete Book of Children's Parties*
- *Complete Book of Wedding Showers*
- *Complete Book of Baby Showers*
- *Complete Book of Wedding Vows*
- *Complete Book of Wedding Toasts*
- *Diane Warner's Wedding Question & Answer Book*
- *How to Have a Big Wedding on a Small Budget, 3rd Edition*
- *Big Wedding on a Small Budget Planner and Organizer*
- *Beautiful Wedding Decorations & Gifts on a Small Budget*
- *Picture-Perfect Worry-Free Weddings: 71 Destinations & Venues*